By Choi Gyu-seok

From the Author:

From the time I vaguely had the idea of drawing a cartoon about the labor movement, I covered it sporadically over several years, going back and forth between determination and giving up countless times.

The labor movement had special stories that could only be found there, and that uniqueness was both a charm and a barrier that attracted me.

Even though I gave up dozens of times because of walls blocking my way, the will, skepticism, optimism and pessimism, glory and hurt of the people I met during my research turned me back from giving up.

I hope this cartoon will be encouraging to the countless people who have inspired me to tell this story even while feeling confused and at a loss.

May 2015

Choi Gyu-seok

1

Volume 1

Story Advisors
Ha Jong-gang,
Kim Kyung-wook,
Lee Seon-ok

Writing Assistance
Jung Pil-won

Foreign Ambassador Reviewer
Kim Nak-ho

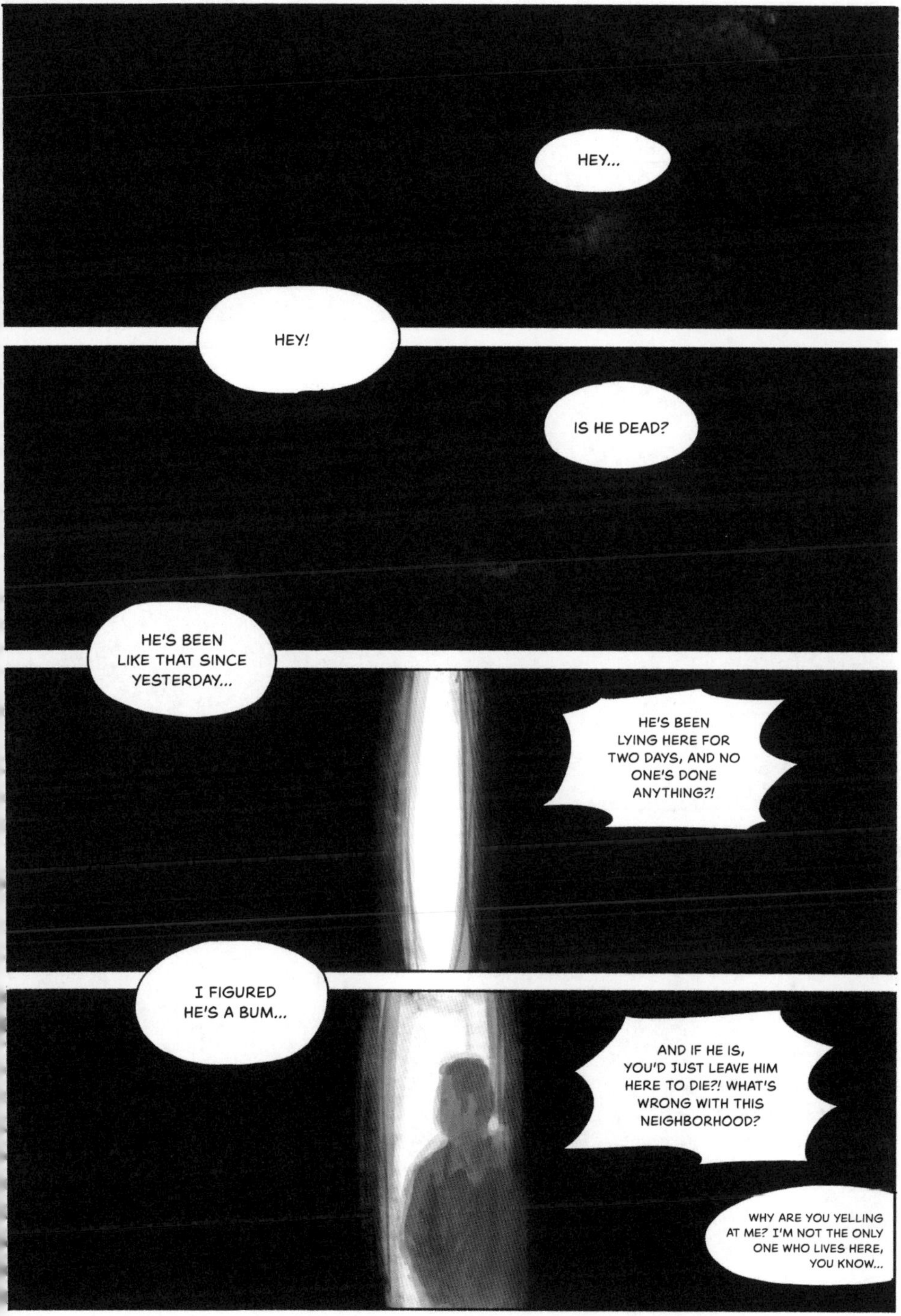
HEY...
HEY!
IS HE DEAD?
HE'S BEEN LIKE THAT SINCE YESTERDAY...
HE'S BEEN LYING HERE FOR TWO DAYS, AND NO ONE'S DONE ANYTHING?!
I FIGURED HE'S A BUM...
AND IF HE IS, YOU'D JUST LEAVE HIM HERE TO DIE?! WHAT'S WRONG WITH THIS NEIGHBORHOOD?
WHY ARE YOU YELLING AT ME? I'M NOT THE ONLY ONE WHO LIVES HERE, YOU KNOW...

HE'S WAKING UP. HE'S NOT DEAD.
HEY, ARE YOU OKAY?
WAKE UP.
YOU LIVE AROUND HERE?
HE'S A BUM...
HAVE YOU EATEN?
CAN'T YOU SPEAK?

I THINK HE MIGHT BE SLOW...
SIR, ARE YOU HERE TO TAKE THIS BOX?
HUH?
EH, WELL... HOW COULD I, UH...
WOW... SO I'M RIGHT!
MAN...
THIS NEIGHBORHOOD'S A JUNGLE.
AH, THAT'S NOT TRUE...

THE WORLD'S CRUEL SOMETIMES. REAL CRUEL.
GRRRMB
YOU HUNGRY? WANNA EAT?
YEAH...
NOM
NOM
SO, YOU'VE BEEN WORKING DELIVERY FOR SIX MONTHS, BUT YOU WERE FIRED BEFORE RECEIVING PAYMENT?
IT'S...BECAUSE I WRECKED THE MOTORBIKE.
ARE YOU SAYING YOU GAVE YOUR PAYCHECK BACK OR THAT YOU NEVER RECEIVED IT?
I... NEVER RECEIVED ANYTHING...
MY BOSS WAS REAL MAD ABOUT THE WRECKED BIKE.
WHERE IS THIS PLACE?

*FRESH TASTE RESTAURANT

THIS GUY WORKED HERE FOR SIX MONTHS, RIGHT?
AH... YES...
HOW MANY PEOPLE WORK HERE?
SIX PEOPLE, NOT INCLUDING THE BOSS.
OKAY.
00:00:23
WHO ARE YOU?
OH, YOU'RE THE BOSS?
??
I SAID THIS BASTARD WOULD DIE IF I SAW HIM AGAIN! WHAT'S HE CRAWLING BACK FOR?!
AH, WELL...
WE CAME HERE TO COLLECT UNPAID WAGES.

UNPAID WAGES?
WHO ARE YOU? WHAT DO YOU HAVE TO DO WITH THIS?
I MET HIM ON THE STREET A LITTLE WHILE AGO.
HEH...
THIS IS CRAZY...
IF ANYTHING, I SHOULD BE GETTING COMPENSATION FOR THE DAMAGES THIS ASSHOLE CAUSED!
GET OUT OF HERE BEFORE I CALL THE COPS FOR DISRUPTION OF BUSINESS!
AH! THE LAW!
YOU LIKE THE LAW, HUH?
VIOLATION OF ARTICLE 36 OF THE LABOR STANDARDS ACT. IMPRISONMENT FOR UP TO THREE YEARS OR A FINE OF UP TO 20 MILLION WON.
ENFORCEMENT DECREE OF THE LABOR STANDARDS ACT. INTEREST FOR LATE PAYMENT OF UNPAID WAGES SHALL BE 20% PER ANNUM.

*ABOUT $5,250 USD AT CURRENT CONVERSION RATE (2024)

I THOUGHT YOU WERE A MAN OF THE LAW...
TAK
TAK
I DON'T USUALLY DO THIS, BUT...
♫ ...YOUR VACANT SEAT... ♪
RINGTONE: "너의 빈자리" (YOUR VACANT SEAT) BY YONG-PIL CHO
HEY, BOSS!
WHAT'S GOING ON?
YOU KNOW THE FRESH TASTE CHINESE RESTAURANT?
YEAH, I KNOW IT. WE HAVE COMPANY DINNERS THERE SOMETIMES.
DO YOU THINK I HAVE NOBODY TO CALL...?
DON'T GO THERE ANYMORE.
OH?
DON'T EAT THERE. DON'T EVEN GET TAKEOUT.

*NOODLES WITH BLACK BEAN SAUCE, POPULAR CHINESE DISH IN SOUTH KOREA

HELLO?
OH, YEAH. I KNOW IT. WE HAD OUR LAUNCH DINNER THERE.
DON'T GO THERE ANYMORE.
IF YOU SAY IT, SO IT GOES. I'LL SPREAD THE WORD!
YES, THIS IS THE HANSHIN ELECTRONICS LABOR UNION.
RING RING
FRESH TASTE? THEIR FOOD'S OKAY... WHAT? DON'T GO ANYMORE? WELL, SURE...
YES, SIR!
SILLA PRECISION BUJIN BRANCH...
OF COURSE. LOYALTY!
FRESH TASTE?
HUH, WELL... IF THE BOSS SAYS SO. I'LL CANCEL OUR RESERVATION.
WHAT POWER DO I HAVE? IF THAT'S THE WORD, WE'RE NOT GOING.
OKAY. I'LL AVOID IT. SEE YOU ON TUESDAY.
LET'S SEE... WHO ELSE IS THERE...?
덥석
GRAB

BUH...
BOSS!
YOU'RE THE BOSS HERE, NOT ME.
MISTER!
I'LL GIVE IT TO YOU! I'LL PAY!
KB
태 산 금속 주방
HERE.
KB
PLEASE PUT IT IN YOUR BAG FOR SAFEKEEPING.

THANK YOU.
THANK YOU SO MUCH.
IT'S IMPORTANT THAT YOU UNDERSTAND...
...AND NOT FORGET WHAT HAPPENED HERE TODAY.
OKAY, THEN. BYE.
AH... I... WAIT A MINUTE...
PLEASE... THIS...
WHAT'S THIS? A REWARD?
IT'S NOT MUCH, BUT...
HOW OLD ARE YOU?
I'M TWENTY-FOUR.
HEY... AT YOUR AGE, YOU GOTTA HANG ON TO EVERYTHING YOU CAN.
BUDDY, DON'T TRY TO IMITATE USELESS ADULTS.
TAKE CARE OF YOUR FOOD BOWL, OKAY?

THERE WE GO.
BYE-BYE.
KB
...
OH!
HERE.
LET ME KNOW IF YOU NEED ANYTHING.
GET BACK YOUR STOLEN WAGES
Bujang Labor Counseling Center
Counseling Director Go-shin Gu
5F, 00-1 Hanma-dong, Wontong-gu, Bujang-si, Gosin-gi, Gyeonggi-do
Phone: (030)555-1234
Fax: (030)555-1232
Mobile: 019-2335-0000
Email: ggsin@amail.com
Backpay / Workers' Comp /
Unfair dismissal / Trade Union

Chapter 1

드르르르르르르르르
WHrrrrrrrr...

위이이이
WRRRRRRR...
HEY, WE CAN'T PUT THAT AWAY YET!
OOPS! SORRY...
JUST KEEP WORKING LIKE THAT.
I'M HEADING OVER HERE!
JEONG-MI, I'VE ASKED YOU NOT TO GIVE ORDERS TO THE OUTSIDE PROMOTORS.
I'M BUSY, SO WHAT ELSE SHOULD I DO? I DID IT LIKE THIS UNDER THE PREVIOUS MANAGER.
NO MATTER WHAT YOU DID BEFORE, YOU SHOULDN'T DO IT HERE AND NOW.
I'VE REPEATED SEVERAL TIMES THAT THE PROMOTORS ARE NOT OUR COMPANY'S EMPLOYEES.

WHAT KIND OF MAN IS SO STRICT?
HE SAID HE WAS A SOLDIER. I WONDER IF HE EVEN LET THE YOUNG GUYS UNDER HIM BREATHE WITHOUT PERMISSION...
MAKES YOU WONDER WHY HE SUPPOSEDLY QUIT SUCH A GOOD JOB IN TIMES LIKE THESE, HUH?
I'LL BET HE GOT KICKED OUT BECAUSE HIS SUBORDINATES FLED OR COMMITTED SUICIDE.
BOSS, THE STORE MANAGER'S COMING!
FOREMAN, PLEASE MOVE THE BOXES TO THE BACK QUICKLY!

OK.*
*GASTON SPEAKS ENGLISH, RATHER THAN KOREAN.
OH, MR. LEE!

WONDERFUL!
FANTASTIC!
MR. JUNG...
TAKE A PHOTO AND SEND IT TO HQ.
YES.
GOOD JOB, SOO-IN. YOU'RE THE BEST.
THANKS, GASTON.
MR. LEE, PLEASE COME TO THE CONFERENCE ROOM LATER.
YES, SIR.

A NEW SUPERMARKET OPENED NEARBY RECENTLY, AND OUR SALES ARE DOWN, SO THE STORE MANAGER IS KEEPING AN EYE OUT.
DO YOUR BEST SO THAT YOU DON'T GET CAUGHT LOOKING IDLE.
IF YOU REQUESTED DAYS OFF, YOU NEED TO DISCUSS IT WITH ME AND REORGANIZE IT.
SIR, I NEED SUNDAY OFF FOR MY NEPHEW'S WEDDING.
I CAN'T JUST CHANGE MY PLANS...
DO YOU THINK THE OUTSIDE PROMOTORS NEVER HAVE WEEKEND PLANS?
SURELY THAT'S NOT THE CASE.
IF YOU KEEP DOING THIS UNFAIRLY, I'LL HAVE TO MANAGE THE HOLIDAY SCHEDULE WITHOUT EMPLOYEE INPUT.
WE'RE ALL IN THE SAME BOAT, SO WE NEED TO MAKE CONCESSIONS FOR EACH OTHER.
YOU WORKED HARD PREPARING FOR OUR OPENING TODAY. COME ON, LET'S FIGHT!

VEGETABLES AND FRUITS!
GO FOR IT!
UGH, REALLY.
IF THE PROMOTORS AREN'T OUR EMPLOYEES, WHY DOES HE ALWAYS DEFEND THEM?
RIGHT? OUR MANAGER SHOULD BE ON OUR SIDE.
LADIES, YOU'LL GET WRINKLES IF YOU GET TOO ANGRY ABOUT IT. THE MANAGER IS NEW. JUST WAIT HIM OUT.
HE HATES EVERYTHING I DO. HOW ELSE AM I SUPPOSED TO FEEL?
AH, MAN... DAYS LIKE THIS, I ALMOST WANT TO FIRE EVERYONE.

TAKE A SEAT.
THIS IS A DIRECTIVE FROM THE STORE MANAGER.
NERVE-RACKING. AN ORDER FROM THE HIGHER-UPS...
YOUR CURRENT SALESPEOPLE...
NO MATTER THE MEANS...
푸르미
Fourmi
...GET THEM ALL OUT.

VEGETABLES AND FRUITS!
GO FOR IT!
...
SIR, WHAT ON EARTH...?
I'M NOT TAKING QUESTIONS.
JUST DO IT.
WHAT?
HOW CAN I...?
SHOULD I HAVE TO TELL YOU THAT?
IT CAN BE THROUGH HARSH WORDS OR DISCIPLINE. JUST MAKE SURE THEY LEAVE ON THEIR OWN.

YOU WERE A MILITARY OFFICER.
THIS SHOULD BE SIMPLE FOR YOU, RIGHT?
PLATOON COMMANDER, LOOK OVER THERE. WH...WHAT SHOULD WE DO?
SHH!

THE SHADOWS OF SEVERAL PEOPLE, CRAWLING LOW TO THE GROUND, WERE APPROACHING FROM THE DMZ TOWARD THE SOUTH...
THE ENEMY.
ABSURDLY, THE FIRST THING THAT CAME TO MIND WAS THE IMAGE OF MYSELF AS A FOUR-STAR GENERAL.
EVEN IN A CRITICAL SITUATION, I WASN'T THE LEAST BIT AFRAID.
I'VE NEVER EVEN BEEN LUCKY ENOUGH TO FIND A 1,000-WON NOTE ON THE ROAD.
SO THIS OPPORTUNITY WAS UNPRECEDENTED.
AS LONG AS THE CLAYMORE MINE DETONATES PROPERLY, THE PROBLEM IS SOLVED JUST LIKE THAT.
SHOULD I TRIGGER IT NOW?
NOW?

THEY DISAPPEARED.
WHERE...?
WHERE?!
WHERE ARE YOU?!

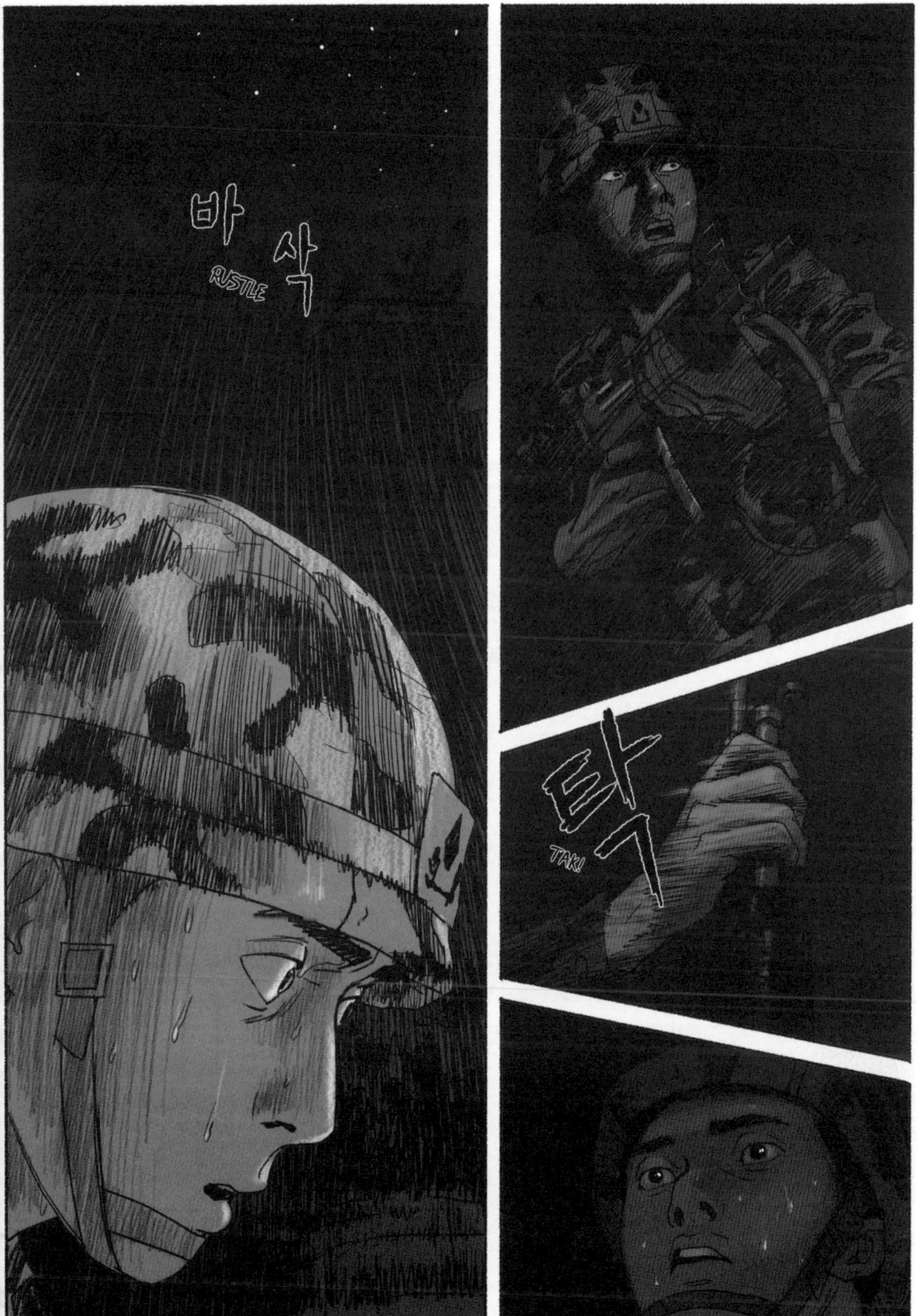

바 삭
RUSTLE
탁
TAK!

PLATOON
COMMANDER?!
IT'S ME!
DON'T SHOOT!

빽
THUD
HEY, ASSHOLE, CAN'T YOU FIND YOUR OWN STATION?
YOU'RE A SERGEANT, AND YOU DON'T EVEN KNOW WHERE THE TRENCHES ARE?! HUH?!
SORRY...
I'M SORRY...
YOU BASTARD. I ALMOST...
WHAT IF I'D KILLED YOU?!
HUH? WHAT WOULD'VE HAPPENED IF I'D TRIGGERED IT...?
ONCE THAT BUTTON'S PRESSED...
A MIXTURE OF GUILT, SHAME, FEAR, AND RELIEF OVERWHELMED ME.
I HAD TWO MOMENTS TO FOLLOW THROUGH, AND I HESITATED BOTH TIMES. I BELIEVED I COULD DO IT, BUT MY BODY WOULDN'T LET ME.
IN THAT MOMENT, I REALIZED THAT I WASN'T CUT OUT FOR A MILITARY CAREER.

THIS ISN'T ANYONE'S LIFE'S WORK, AND THERE'S A LOT OF TURNOVER ANYWAY.
IF YOU GIVE THEM A LITTLE PUSH, THEY'LL LEAVE ON THEIR OWN.
...AND NOW I REALIZE THAT I'M NOT CUT OUT TO BE A COMPANY MAN, EITHER.
SIR...
THAT'S...
...ILLEGAL.
RECEIVE ORDERS, EXECUTE.
THAT FAMILIAR AND NATURAL REPETITION IS BROKEN.
LIKE A CLUMSY BUTCHER WHO MESSES UP ON CLEANLY KILLING THE CHICKEN AND DOESN'T KNOW WHAT TO DO NEXT.

I CAN'T DO THAT.
I SEE...
YOU CAN GO.

ANYTHING TO WRAP?
I WAS JUST ABOUT TO DO IT.
WHY?
GOOD WORK.
I'LL TAKE CARE OF IT. YOU HEAD BACK OUT TO THE FLOOR.

THAT'S ILLEGAL, SIR. YOU KNOW THAT, RIGHT?
YOU IDIOT...
WHAT ARE YOU, A LAWYER? A LABOR ATTORNEY?
DO YOU EVEN KNOW WHAT THE LAW SAYS?
I WONDER HOW I BECAME THIS KIND OF PERSON.
COMING HERE WON'T RESOLVE YOUR ISSUE.
YOU NEED TO LEAVE.
WE'RE WORKERS, HERE TO COLLECT OUR WAGES. WHY WOULD YOU BLOCK US?!
THERE'S NO REFUSAL TO PAY. IT'S JUST A DELAY. UNDERSTAND?
IT'S ILLEGAL FOR YOU TO GATHER OUTSIDE LIKE THIS.

LOOK HERE, KID!
HEY... WHAT D'YOU MEAN "KID"?
ARE YOU A POLICE OFFICER OR A COMPANY GUARD DOG?!
YOU'RE CLEARLY IN HAN-BONG JANG'S POCKET, YOU BASTARD!
STOP US AGAIN, AND I'LL STRIP THAT UNIFORM FROM YOU MYSELF!
IF YOU DON'T WANT THE TROUBLE, GET OUT OF THE WAY.
THIS...
SIR... AT LEAST LEAVE THAT STUFF HERE.
WHAT, THIS?
THIS IS MY LIVELIHOOD!
WHAT ARE YOU DOING?
LET'S GO!

HAN-BONG JANG!
WHERE IS HAN-BONG JANG, PRESIDENT OF HANBONG CONSTRUCTION?
WHO... WHO ARE YOU?
ME? YOU DON'T EVEN KNOW WHO WORKS FOR YOU?
LET'S NOT DO THIS HERE...
...SNOOZE...
WE NEED TO SEE HAN-BONG JANG!
EH?!
WHAT ARE YOU JUST STANDING THERE FOR?
DON'T WANNA GET PAID?
I, UH... I WONDER IF THIS IS OKAY...
HELLO, EVERYONE...
YOU DON'T NEED THE PLEASANTRIES!

WH... WHAT'S GOING ON?
WHAT'S THE PROBLEM?
WE'RE HERE FOR OUR WAGES. THE CONSTRUCTION PROJECT'S BEEN FINISHED FOR AGES. WHY HAVEN'T YOU PAID US?
YOU... YOU THUGS CAME ALL THE WAY HERE...!
DON'T YOU KNOW WHO MY SON IS?!
YOUR SON'S A MEMBER OF THE NATIONAL ASSEMBLY. DOES THAT GIVE YOU THE RIGHT TO ROB US?
STIFFING PEOPLE LIKE THIS... YOU'RE SMEARING SHIT ON YOUR SON'S REPUTATION!
DO YOU HEAR THE WAY THIS MAN'S TALKING?!

WHAT ARE YOU DOING?
GET THIS THUG OUT OF HERE!
GET HIM OUT OF MY SIGHT RIGHT NOW!
NOW!
UH...MAYBE WE SHOULD LEAVE.

꽈앙
BANG
가가가가각
SCRAAAAAPE

SEE THIS LINE?
IF YOU'VE GOT THE BALLS, COME AND CROSS IT.
YOU'LL SEE WHAT HAPPENS.
MR. PRESIDENT!
MISS KIM...
IMMEDIATELY... WRITE UP THE PAYMENTS AND SEND THESE MEN ON THEIR WAY.

A REAL MAN SAYS WHAT HE HAS TO SAY, EVEN IF HE HAS A KNIFE AT HIS THROAT.
I'VE NEVER LOWERED MY EYES IN FRONT OF SOMEONE MORE POWERFUL THAN ME. UNDERSTAND?
PERHAPS I INHERITED THE THING MY FATHER VALUED MOST IN HIMSELF: HIS PRIDE.
PEOPLE HAVE NO CONSCIOUS THESE DAYS.
WE WERE PICKING CHESTNUTS, AND EVERYONE FOUND A WAY TO STEAL SOME FOR THEMSELVES.
PEOPLE EVEN TOOK A POUND OR TWO HOME WITH THEM.
MOM, COULDN'T YOU HAVE DONE THE SAME?
WHAT ARE YOU SAYING? THAT'D BE STEALING.
IT'S BETTER TO LIVE HONESTLY IN POVERTY THAN TO BE WEALTHY AND SINFUL.
AND MAYBE I INHERITED MY MOTHER'S SENSITIVITY, TOO AFRAID TO HOE FOR FEAR OF HURTING AN EARTHWORM.

HEY, ARE YOU CRAZY?
HUH?
NO... NO, SIR.
SHUT UP! CAN'T YOU SEE YOUR CLASSMATES ARE STUDYING?!
빡
SMACK
YOU THINK YOU'RE TOUGH, HUH?
YOU WANNA CHALLENGE ME?
I ASKED YOU A QUESTION, ASSHOLE. WHY DON'T YOU ANSWER?

IN ANY CASE, I'VE ALWAYS BEEN SOMEONE'S STUMBLING BLOCK.

HEY, PIL-GEUN JEONG...
CUT IT OUT.
WHAT D'YOU WANT?
DO YOU THINK YOU'RE ALLOWED TO HIT SOMEONE JUST BECAUSE YOU'RE A YEAR OLDER?
DID THIS GUY TAKE A BLOW TO THE HEAD?!
콰당
CLATTER
SLIIIDE
HEY...
WHAT'S ALL THE NOISE?

SOO-IN LEE, I TOLD YOU TO KEEP AN EYE ON THE CLASS DURING STUDY HOUR. ARE YOU MAKING A FUSS?
COME WITH ME!
빡 SMACK
빡 SMACK
빡 SMACK
빡 SMACK
빡 SMACK
OUR HOMEROOM TEACHER'S NICKNAME WAS "BLACK HOLE."
I'D BEEN TRAMPLED BY HIM SINCE THE BEGINNING OF THE SCHOOL YEAR.
CLASS REPRESENTATIVE...
THE CLASSROOM'S SO BARE. WOULDN'T IT BE NICE TO HAVE A FISH TANK?

HEY?
CLASS REP...
...
THE TEACHER'S
TALKING TO YOU...
ARE YOU DEAF
OR SOMETHING?
HEY,
SOO-IN LEE...
툭 툭
POKE POKE
쿡
POKE
쿡
POKE
MY FAMILY
DOESN'T HAVE MONEY
FOR THAT.
WHAT...?
WELL,
THERE YOU GO...
THIS KID IS
COMPLETELY
MESSED UP!
짝
SMACK
철썩
SLAP
WHEN DID I ASK
FOR MONEY?!
짝
SMACK
WHEN, HUH?
YOU BASTARD!

FROM THAT DAY ON, I GOT HIT WHENEVER HE FOUND THE CHANCE.
INITIALLY, SINCE THERE WERE 55 OTHER STUDENTS SUFFERING THE SAME TREATMENT, IT WAS BEARABLE.
BY THE SECOND SEMESTER, HOWEVER, HIS TARGETS NARROWED TO ME AND PIL-GEUN.
AFTER PIL-GEUN'S MOM BOUGHT A FISH TANK, THOUGH, I BECAME THE SOLE TARGET.
THE INTENSITY OF MY TEACHER'S BLOWS WERE PROPORTIONAL TO HIS SWEAT.
AS IF IT WERE HONEST LABOR THAT PAID OFF.
HE WAS LIKE A FARMER THRESHING RICE, WITH THE AWARENESS THAT THE HARVEST DEPENDED ON HIS EFFORTS.

I'M SORRY THAT I HAVEN'T MET WITH YOU UNTIL NOW. WE'VE JUST BEEN SO BUSY...
LIFE'S LIKE THAT SOMETIMES. MAKE YOURSELF COMFORTABLE.
MY MOTHER, NOTICING HER SON'S SUFFERING, SHOWED UP AT SCHOOL.
HEHEHEH...
THE TEACHER'S BEATINGS ONLY STOPPED AFTER SEVERAL DAYS' WORTH OF WAGES WERE LOST TO THE BLACK HOLE.

?
MOM!
DIDN'T YOU GO TO WORK TODAY?
SOO-IN, YOU'RE HOME?
I HURT MY BACK. THAT'S ALL...
THERE'S FOOD. HAVE SOME DINNER.

SHOULD WE GO TO THE HOSPITAL?
FOR WHAT?
IF I GO, THEY'LL JUST TELL ME TO GO HOME AND REST.
WHILE I FORGED AHEAD IN EATING RICE, I COULD BARELY SWALLOW.
I FELT THE VAGUE DESIRE TO GAIN SUCCESS IN LIFE.
AT THAT TIME, MOST OF THE SUCCESSFUL PEOPLE SEEN ON TELEVISION WERE GRADUATES OF THE MILITARY ACADEMY.

*ABSENTEE VOTING

**BATTALION COMMANDER

HOWEVER, WE'RE IN A SPECIAL SITUATION. YOU'RE AWARE THAT THERE ARE THOSE IN THE REPUBLIC OF KOREA WHO STILL ADMIRE AND PRAISE THE NORTH. WE CAN'T ALLOW THIS COUNTRY, BUILT BY THE HARD WORK OF OUR PREDECESSORS, TO FALL INTO THE HANDS OF SUCH FOOLS.
LET'S LEAVE DEMOCRACY TO THE COMMON PEOPLE. WE IN THE MILITARY MUST BE ALERT AND MAINTAIN BALANCE.
THE REASON JAPAN HAS DEVELOPED SO MUCH AND MAINTAINED STRONG SOCIAL STABILITY FOR SO LONG...
투표용지 · 선거공보*
ISN'T IT BECAUSE THE LIBERAL DEMOCRATIC PARTY HAS BEEN IN POWER FOR A LONG TIME?
*ELECTION BALLOT
I'M NOT PRESSING YOU TO VOTE FOR ANYONE IN PARTICULAR. THAT WOULDN'T BE FAIR.
I'M ONLY GIVING YOU ADVICE AS A SUPERIOR WITH MORE LIFE EXPERIENCE, TO ALLOW YOU TO MAKE BETTER DECISIONS.

I TRUST YOU'LL CHOOSE WISELY...
SEND IN THE NEXT PERSON AS YOU LEAVE.
YES, SIR!
I WILL DO MY DUTY.
Cadet Code of Honor
We dedicate our lives to our country and our people.
We always live with honor and faithfulness.
We choose the difficult path of justice over the easy path of injustice.
GO ON IN.
HUH? SOO-IN, YOU'RE NOT VOTING?
NO.

IT'S CLEARLY A FORM OF ELECTION FRAUD!
WE SHOULDN'T JUST IGNORE IT...
THERE'S A PRESIDENTIAL ELECTION AT THE END OF THE YEAR, SO WON'T IT BE EVEN WORSE THEN?!
AS 4TH-YEAR STUDENTS, WE SHOULD REPORT THIS.
WHAT IF WE GET PULLED INTO A HUGE MESS?
THE STUDENT BODY ASSEMBLY IS IN TWO DAYS, RIGHT?
COULD WE FOLD IT INTO THE AGENDA?
RATHER THAN JUST A FEW OF US COMING FORWARD, WE CAN RALLY THE WHOLE CLASS.
IF YOU BRING IT UP SUDDENLY, WON'T EVERYONE REJECT IT?
WE'LL INFORM EVERYONE IN ADVANCE. GIVEN OUR OWN REACTIONS, I'M SURE IT'LL BE APPRECIATED.
I THINK EVERYONE MUST BE REALLY SHOCKED BY THIS.

WHAT'S THE STAFF STILL DOING HERE...?
WHAT? EVEN THE PRINCIPAL'S HERE?
HOW DID THEY KNOW...?
WHAT DO WE DO NOW? DO WE GO THROUGH WITH IT?

LET'S...
LET'S BEGIN THE
STUDENT ASSEMBLY.
FIRST OF ALL,
WE WILL SWEAR
FAITHFULNESS...
REGARDING THE
CADET DAY EVENT...
...PLEASE ASSURE YOUR
OUTSIDE GUESTS ARE
DRESSED APPROPRIATELY.
NOW, WE'LL
DISCUSS PREPARATIONS
FOR SUMMER MILITARY
EXERCISES...

IF THERE'S NO OTHER TOPIC FOR DISCUSSION, THIS WILL CONCLUDE THE MEETING.
WITHOUT EVEN REALIZING...
...I HAD ALREADY PUT MY HAND UP.
AH... YES... CADET SOO-IN LEE.
PL...PLEASE SPEAK.

THE MILITARY MUST MAINTAIN POLITICAL NEUTRALITY AND DEFEND DEMOCRACY.
OVER THE PAST THREE YEARS, I'VE HAD THIS PHRASE ETCHED INTO MY BONES THROUGH REPETITION.
IT IS ALSO A PRINCIPLE WE MUST TEACH WHEN WE STAND BEFORE OUR SOLDIERS AS OFFICERS NEXT YEAR.
ALL OF THAT SAID...
AT THIS MILITARY ACADEMY THAT TRAINS ELITE OFFICERS, AN INCIDENT HAS OCCURRED THAT'S VIOLATED POLITICAL NEUTRALITY AND INTERFERED IN AN ELECTION.

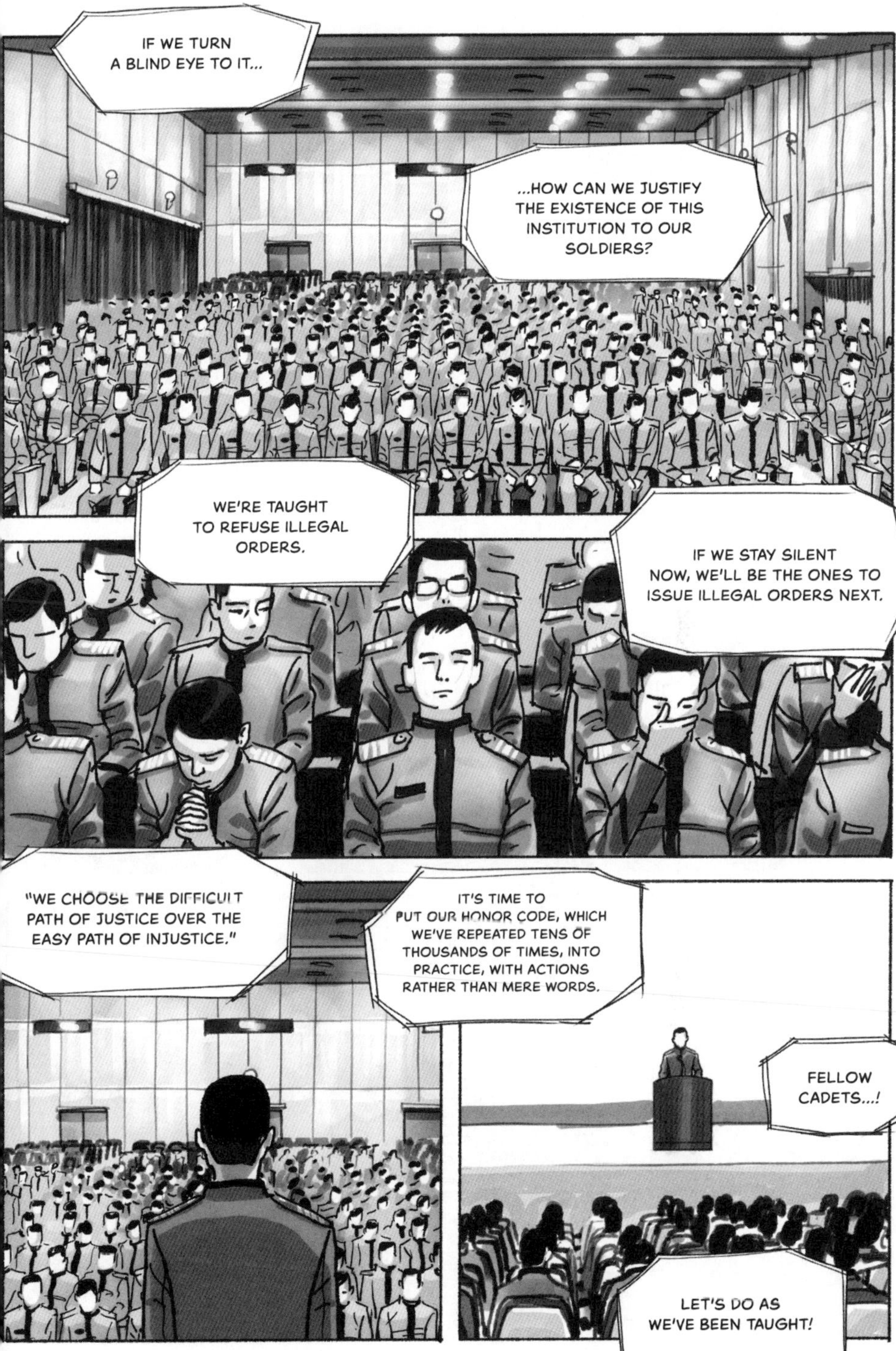
IF WE TURN A BLIND EYE TO IT...
...HOW CAN WE JUSTIFY THE EXISTENCE OF THIS INSTITUTION TO OUR SOLDIERS?
WE'RE TAUGHT TO REFUSE ILLEGAL ORDERS.
IF WE STAY SILENT NOW, WE'LL BE THE ONES TO ISSUE ILLEGAL ORDERS NEXT.
"WE CHOOSE THE DIFFICULT PATH OF JUSTICE OVER THE EASY PATH OF INJUSTICE."
IT'S TIME TO PUT OUR HONOR CODE, WHICH WE'VE REPEATED TENS OF THOUSANDS OF TIMES, INTO PRACTICE, WITH ACTIONS RATHER THAN MERE WORDS.
FELLOW CADETS...!
LET'S DO AS WE'VE BEEN TAUGHT!

THAT'S ALL.
AFTER THAT ROUGH, THEORETICAL SPEECH...
...THERE WAS SILENCE FOR A WHILE.
JUST WHEN THAT SILENCE BEGAN TO INSTILL A VAGUE FEAR IN ME...
...FROM CORNERS OF THE AUDITORIUM...
CLAP
...SLOWLY, THERE BEGAN...
CLAP
...A SHY CHORUS OF APPLAUSE.
EH-HEM...
짝
CLAP
짝
CLAP
짝
CLAP
짝
CLAP

SOO-IN LEE, YOU CRAZY BASTARD!
WHAT DID YOU INTEND TO SAY WITH THAT SPEECH, YOU IDIOT?!
WHILE I WAS SUFFERING THE OUTRAGE OF THE DISCIPLINE OFFICER, WHO HAD ALWAYS PROVED HIMSELF A CALM AND COMPOSED MAN...
...THE VAGUE FEAR I FELT EARLIER SOLIDIFIED INTO CONCRETE TERROR.
YOU WANT TO PLAY HERO?! DO YOU THINK YOU'LL STILL BE ABLE TO ATTEND THIS ACADEMY?!
KNOW THAT THERE ARE A MILLION WAYS TO BE EXPELLED!!
EXPELLED...

A REAL MAN SAYS WHAT HE HAS TO SAY, EVEN IF HE HAS A KNIFE AT HIS THROAT.
I THINK I'D PREFER THE KNIFE.
FEAR AND PAIN DISAPPEAR AFTER A MOMENT.
WHAT COMES AFTER THIS FIGURATIVE KNIFE, HOWEVER...
MY PARENTS WILL HAVE TO PRETEND THAT THEY'RE UNDERSTANDING OF MY SITUATION.
MAYBE IT'LL LAST A LIFETIME...
I'LL HAVE TO PRETEND THAT I DON'T SEE THEIR SIGHS, REGRET, AND SELF-REPROACH.
RATHER THAN LIVING A PREDETERMINED LIFE WHERE ALL I NEED TO DO IS RUN ON RAILS...
I'LL BE ON THE STARTING LINE, ANXIOUS, WITH NO IDEA WHERE I'LL END UP.
I'LL HAVE TO SACRIFICE A LOT TO EARN MONEY FOR TUITION AND LIVING EXPENSES THAT I WAS PREVIOUSLY GIVEN FOR FREE.

I'D BE IN AN UNFAMILIAR SPACE, RUNNING LATE, SCRAMBLING TO GET TO WORK...
EVERYTHING TEDIOUS, DRAINING, UNCERTAIN... ENDURING LONG HOURS IN EXCHANGE FOR BEING A MAN FOR ONE MINUTE, LIKE HAVING TO DO THREE YEARS OF MILITARY SERVICE AGAIN.
MY FATHER, WHO HAD NOTHING TO LOSE BUT HIS PRIDE, NEVER TOLD ME WHAT I COULD LOSE ON THE OTHER SIDE OF THE KNIFE.
...
...
...
...

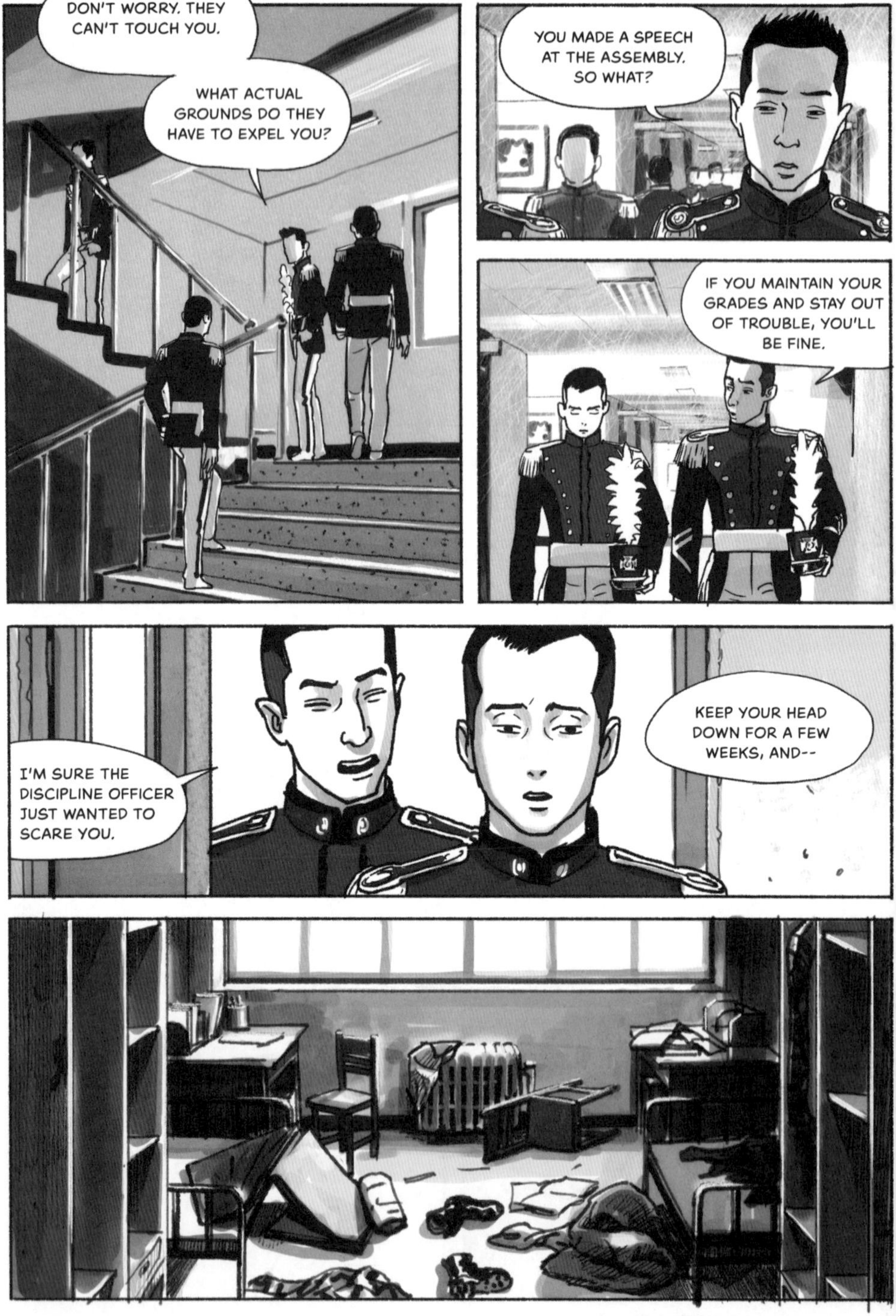
DON'T WORRY. THEY CAN'T TOUCH YOU.
WHAT ACTUAL GROUNDS DO THEY HAVE TO EXPEL YOU?
YOU MADE A SPEECH AT THE ASSEMBLY. SO WHAT?
IF YOU MAINTAIN YOUR GRADES AND STAY OUT OF TROUBLE, YOU'LL BE FINE.
I'M SURE THE DISCIPLINE OFFICER JUST WANTED TO SCARE YOU.
KEEP YOUR HEAD DOWN FOR A FEW WEEKS, AND--

EH?! WH-WHAT HAPPENED?!
-POOR BED ARRANGM
-POOR MAINTENENCE
WEAPONS
-POOR DESK CLEANLINESS
-POOR ROOM CLEANLINESS
-POOR CLEANLINESS OF
WARDROBE
HOW...HOW MANY ARE THERE?
ONE, TWO...
...THREE, FOUR ...
-POOR CLEANLINESS
WARDROBE
-INTRODUCTION OF
SEDICIOUS MATERIA
-INTENTIONAL
OF DIVISION
...EIGHT, NINE...
SEDITIOUS MATERIALS?!

...
쿵
THUD...
FOUR-TEEN.
TEN DEMERITS FOR EACH INFRACTION...
A PENALTY OF 140 POINTS...
I'M TOAST...
NO WAY!
RESPONSIBILITY FOR CADET QUARTERS IS A SHARED RESPONSIBILITY, SO LET'S SPLIT IT UP!
THAT WAY, WE'LL TAKE 70 DEMERITS EACH.

DID THE DISCIPLINE OFFICER MAKE A MISTAKE IN COUNTING THE INFRACTIONS?
IN ANY CASE, IT'S ONLY A MATTER OF TIME...
HEY! SOO-IN LEE!
UH...
EH?
HUH?
빠
CRACK!
각

CADET SOO-IN LEE!
SIR!
AH... RELAX. JUST STAY IN BED.
LET'S SEE... LOOKS LIKE YOU'LL BE ADMITTED HERE FOR ABOUT A MONTH TO REST.
ONCE YOU'RE DISCHARGED, YOU'LL HAVE TO USE CRUTCHES FOR A MONTH OR TWO.
UH...
WHAT'S UP?
IS SOMETHING WRONG?
WELL...
COULD YOU PLEASE DELAY MY DISCHARGE FOR AS LONG AS POSSIBLE?

UHM...
HMM...
ALRIGHT. WE'LL FIGURE IT OUT.
SINCE THE HOSPITAL'S AFFILIATED WITH THE ACADEMY, THEY WON'T ARGUE TOO MUCH.
IF YOU'RE IN FOR A COUPLE OF MONTHS, THEN IT'LL BE WINTER BREAK... THE DUST WILL HAVE SETTLED BY THEN, RIGHT?
OH, THANK YOU!
YOU DID A GOOD THING. YOU KNOW THAT, RIGHT?
OH? DO YOU REGRET IT?
REGRET...
YEAH, MAYBE.

RATHER...
I'M SCARED I'LL DO SOMETHING I REALLY REGRET NEXT TIME.
HEHEHE...
DO YOU LOOK DOWN ON KOREA THAT MUCH?
THIS COUNTRY IS NOT SO LAX AS TO ALLOW YOU TO GROW OLD WITH THE MENTALITY YOU HAVE NOW.
JUST WAIT A FEW YEARS... SOONER OR LATER, YOU TOO WILL BECOME A NO-NONSENSE OLD MAN.
UNDER DIFFERENT CIRCUMSTANCES, I PROBABLY WOULD'VE BEEN DISGUSTED BY THE DOCTOR'S WORDS, BUT THEY FELT STRANGELY COMFORTING AT THAT TIME.

I HOPED FOR A DAY WHEN I COULD EXIST IN THE WORLD WITHOUT DESPISING MYSELF.
IT WAS OF SOME COMFORT THAT, IF I BECAME A MORALLY POOR ADULT, IT WASN'T MY FAULT AND IT WASN'T A BIG DEAL.
IT MIGHT BE EMBARRASSING TO PROCLAIM IT AS A FUTURE ASPIRATION...
...BUT I DECIDED THAT, ONCE I WAS OVER THIS CRISIS, I'D DO MY BEST TO BECOME AN OLD MAN.
내생명 조국을위해
MY DREAM FOR THE FUTURE: OLD MAN.

?
AAGH!
SIR!
OTHER HAND.
SIR!
SIT DOWN.

YOU SHOULD COME BACK TO THE ACADEMY.
IT'S... IT'S THE DOCTOR'S DECISION.
IT'S OUT OF MY HANDS...
I'VE ALREADY TALKED TO THE DOCTOR.
...
WHERE'S THE COURAGE THAT ALLOWED YOU TO CALL OUT A 3-STAR GENERAL?
YOU WON'T BE EXPELLED, SO COME BACK.

BUT... BUT HOW?
BLACKMAIL.
I TOLD THEM THAT EXPELLING YOU WOULD DO NOTHING BUT GET MEDIA ATTENTION, WHICH WOULD ONLY MAKE THE SITUATION WORSE.
THAT CONVINCED THEM.
AH...
THANK YOU.
I SHOULD THANK ***YOU.***
AS A MEMBER OF THE MILITARY AND AN EDUCATOR, I'M EMBARRASSED.
AND I'M GRATEFUL THAT YOU FOLLOWED THE HONOR CODE YOU WERE TAUGHT.
IF NO CADETS HAD COME FORWARD...
...MAYBE... I'D HAVE BECOME TRULY DISILLUSIONED WITH MY WORK.

WE ALSO...
WHEN IT WAS PROPOSED, WE REFUSED IT...
...THE GIVING OF EDUCATIONAL DIRECTION REGARDING GENERAL ELECTIONS.
ALL THE DISCIPLINE OFFICERS REFUSED...
...SO THE BATTALION COMMANDER DID IT HIMSELF.

SO, I HOPE YOU'RE NO TOO QUICK TO HATE THE MILITARY.
WHY DID I RECEIVE ALL THE DEMERITS, THEN?
THAT WAS PART OF THE FACADE.
AS A TEACHER, I WANTED TO SHOW YOU THE DANGER IN THE SYSTEM.
A BRAVE SOLDIER WHO KNOWS NO FEAR...
...WILL DIE WORTHLESSLY BEFORE THE BATTLE'S EVEN BEGUN.
I HOPE YOU LIVE A LONG TIME.

YOU PROTECTED YOUR HONOR AND THAT OF YOUR CLASSMATES, WHO ARE ALSO MY STUDENTS.
WE WON THIS BATTLE, SO RETURN WITH YOUR HEAD HELD HIGH.
HE WAS THE MOST RESPECTABLE ADULT I'D EVER MET. LOOKING BACK, HOWEVER... PERHAPS HE WAS THE MOST CUNNING DEFENDER OF THE SYSTEM.
WITH JUST A FEW WORDS, HE HAD RESTORED MY SELF-ESTEEM, SOOTHED MY ANGER TOWARDS THE ACADEMY, AND MADE ME ACCEPT THE UNFAIR PUNISHMENT. ALL WHILE THE SCHOOL DIDN'T CHANGE OR LOSE ANYTHING AT ALL. AND I MISSED THE OPPORTUNITY TO BECOME AN ORDINARY OLD MAN.

ASSEMBLE!!
HEHE... DONG-YOON'S ENJOYING HIS DRILL DUTIES, HUH?
환 육사00기 신임소대장 환열식 영
우루루루루
RUSHHH
HEY, HEY! GET MOVING!
HEADS TO THE GROUND.
RIGHT NOW!!

SOO-IN LEE, WHAT ARE YOU DOING?
SECOND LIEUTENANT SOO-IN LEE!
THE SOLDIERS ARE WATCHING.
BEATINGS AND HARSH PRACTICES SHOULD NOT BE ENCOURAGED!
HEY, ASSHOLES! YOU'RE SUPPOSED TO BE LIEUTENANTS?! AREN'T YOU ASHAMED?!
OOF.

IT MAY BE HARD TO BELIEVE, BUT I ENJOYED THE MILITARY.
IT SEEMED LIKE A SIMPLE WORLD WHERE THERE WERE CLEAR RULES AND INSTRUCTIONS TO FOLLOW, AND FOLLOWING THEM ASSURED REWARDS.
최우수 소대장
최우수 소대장
I BELIEVED THAT FOR A WHILE.
I DISMISSED THAT COMPANY BECAUSE THEIR SANITARY STANDARDS WERE POOR, BUT THE COMMANDER DEMANDED I CONTRACT THEM AGAIN.
THERE MUST BE SOME REASON BEHIND IT.
SOO-IN.
DID I BECOME A LIEUTENANT TO FEED MY SOLDIERS ROTTEN BREAD?
PEOPLE LIKE "BLACK HOLE" WERE EVERYWHERE.

SIR!
CAPTAIN, WHY ARE YOU OUT HERE?
DID YOU GET A RECEIPT?
AH, YES. I'LL SUBMIT IT LATER.
GIVE IT TO ME. I NEED TO CHECK IT.
UH... CHECK? WHAT FOR...?
BECAUSE IT'S WITHIN THE RULES FOR ME TO DO SO.
HAS YOUR WORK NEVER BEEN CHECKED?
SERGEANT MAJOR PARK... WHY DON'T THE NUMBERS MATCH THE INVENTORY?
AH...
IT SAYS HERE THAT TWENTY COMPRESSORS HAVE BEEN DELIVERED, BUT THERE ARE ONLY TEN.
I... I DON'T KNOW. YOU'D HAVE TO ASK THE BATTALION COMMANDER.

EH. WHAT?
I PLACED THE ORDER. IS THERE A PROBLEM?
TO FOLLOW THROUGH... THE DOCUMENTATION WOULD NEED TO BE FALSIFIED.
AND...?
WHAT'S THE PROBLEM?
IF THERE'S NOTHING ELSE, YOU CAN GO. DO YOUR JOB AND POST A REPORT.

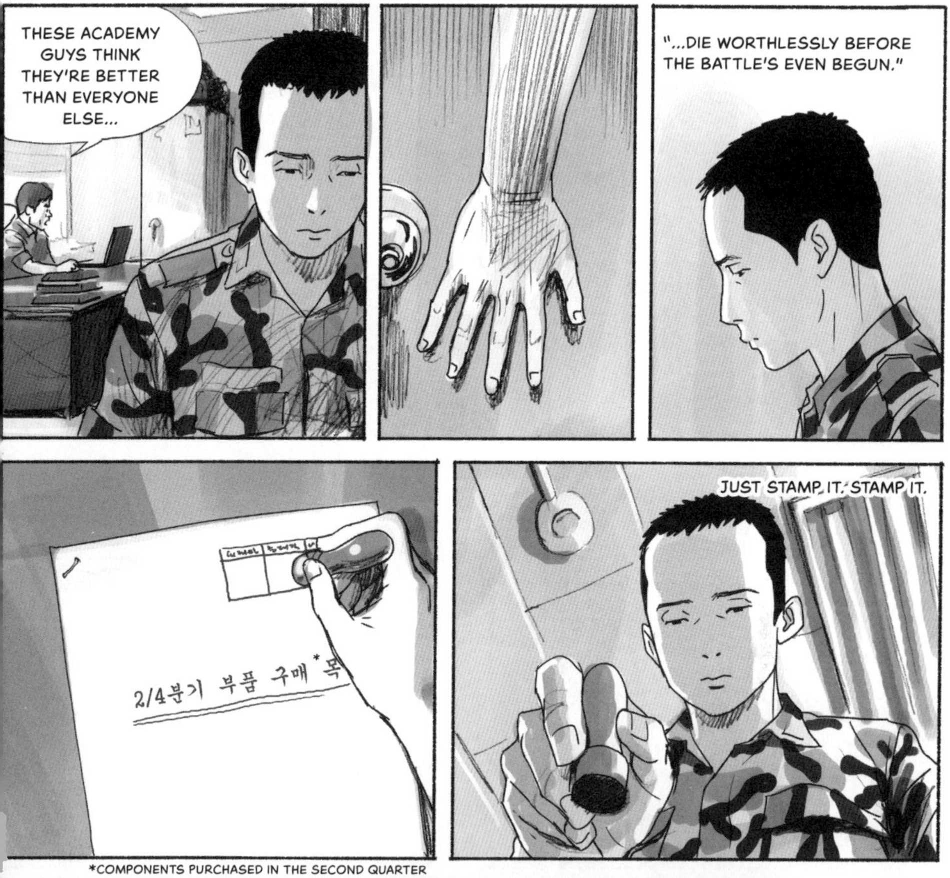

*COMPONENTS PURCHASED IN THE SECOND QUARTER

CAPTAIN LEE, WHAT'S TROUBLING YOU?
AH, SERGEANT MAJOR OH...
HMM...
IF IT'S DIFFICULT FOR YOU TO SIGN THIS, I'LL DO IT FOR YOU.
AH...
SHOULD I NOT?
ALTERNATIVELY, YOU CAN ALWAYS REPORT THE LIEUTENANT COLONEL TO THE MILITARY POLICE.
UH... NO...
WELL, THEN, LET'S GET IT STAMPED.

*REQUEST FOR LEAVE

*BANNER: LET'S SAVE OUR GOLD IN THE CLOSET AND REVIVE THE COUNTRY'S ECONOMY.

THE COMPANY DIDN'T FALL FAR SHORT OF MY EXPECTATIONS.
THE FRENCH WERE NOT UNCOMFORTABLE WITH MY UNIQUENESS AND SEEMED TO SEE IT AS AN ADVANTAGE.
IT WAS A PLACE WHERE EVEN A SALESPERSON WITH ONLY A HIGH SCHOOL DIPLOMA COULD BECOME A MANAGER.
EVERYONE SUFFERED EQUALLY FROM POOR PAY AND HARD WORK.
WHILE HUNDREDS OF OTHERS LEFT THE COMPANY BECAUSE THEY COULDN'T STAND THIS MANNER OF FAIRNESS...
...I QUIETLY TOOK ROOT THERE.

WHAT'S TAKING SO LONG?
DID YOU INVITE SOMEONE ELSE?
MR. PARK.
MR. PARK? FROM JINSONG FOOD?
OH, MY... SORRY I'M LATE.
EVERYONE'S ALREADY HERE.
MR. PARK, I HEARD YOU RECENTLY HAD SURGERY. CAN YOU DRINK?
I'D BETTER BE ABLE TO AFTER PAYING SO MUCH FOR REPAIRS.
BESIDES, IF I TURN YOU DOWN, WOULD FOURMIS CONTINUE TO SELL OUR PRODUCTS?
WOW, MR. PARK, WHAT DO YOU TAKE ME FOR? I'M A LOYAL FRIEND.
LOYAL FRIENDS ALSO NEED TO EAT AND DRINK.
HAHAHA!
OF COURSE, THERE WERE OCCASIONAL TROUBLES HERE, TOO.
SORRY, BUT I HAVE TO GO.
OH? YOU'RE LEAVING ALREADY?
HERE, LET ME GIVE YOU SOME MONEY FOR THE DRINKS...

DON'T MAKE IT UNCOMFORTABLE. GO ON. YOU CAN PAY YOUR CAB FARE.
NO. I ONLY PAID FOR WHAT I ORDERED...
HEY, LEE! PLAYING INNOCENT AT YOUR AGE IS A CRIME!
SIR, AREN'T YOU OVERDOING IT?
DO YOU KNOW HOW MANY BUYERS MY COMPANY LOST WHILE I WAS LAID UP AT THE HOSPITAL?
IF I DON'T DO WHAT I CAN TO KEEP THE REST, I'LL HAVE TO HANG MYSELF.
NOW... LET'S REALLY TEST HOW WELL MY REPAIRS HOLD UP!
BY NOW, I'VE AT LEAST LEARNED ONE THING. IF I CLOSE MY EYES AND TURN AWAY, I CAN PROTECT MYSELF.

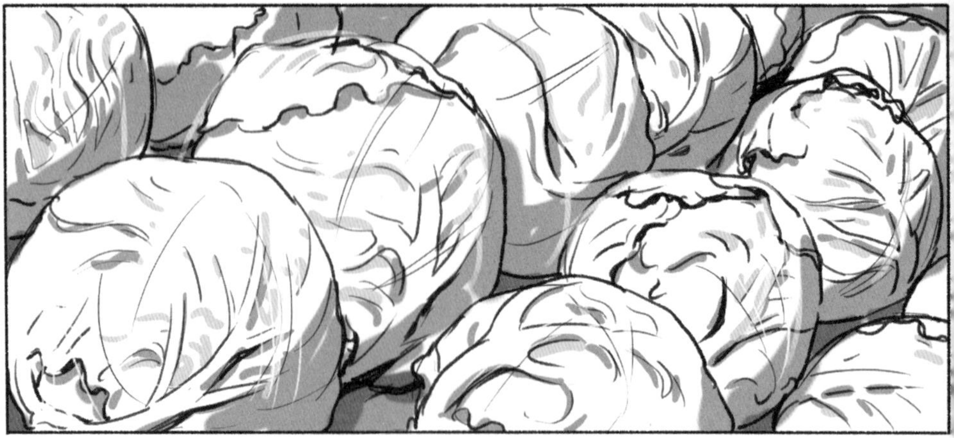

IN THIS PLACE...

...CLOSING MY EYES...

...STAYING QUIET...

...I BELIEVED I COULD CLOSE THE DISTANCE BETWEEN MYSELF AND THE WORLD.

HEADBAND SLOGAN: "FIGHT UNITE

IT DOESN'T MAKE SENSE! DEMANDING WE CUT SO MANY PEOPLE SO QUICKLY...
I'M NOT A SOCIOPATH, YOU KNOW...
SO YOU TOLD HIM YOU'RE AGAINST IT?
WELL, NO... IN FRONT OF THE MANAGER, I... I FOLDED.
IN ANY CASE, IF WE HAVE TO DOWNSIZE, WHY MAKE US DO IT THIS WAY INSTEAD OF FIRING THEM DIRECTLY?
DO YOU THINK ACTUAL LAYOFF PROCEDURES ARE SIMPLE? THIS IS QUICKER AND CHEAPER FOR THE COMPANY.
IT'S STILL NO GOOD. THIS WAY, THE STORE ATMOSPHERE WILL DETERIORATE AND SALES WILL DROP. WE STILL LOSE.

SO, WILL YOU DO IT?
HOW CAN HE?
...
IS THERE ANY ALTERNATIVE?
AREN'T YOU ANGRY, AT LEAST?
IF YOU WASH YOUR HANDS BEFORE WIELDING THE KNIFE, WILL IT STOP YOU FROM GETTING BLOOD ON THEM?
OUR BEING ANGRY NOW IS JUST TO SOOTHE OURSELVES.
WE CAN SAY WE DON'T WANT TO, BUT WE'LL FOLLOW ORDERS ANYWAY.
YOU DIDN'T EVEN RAISE YOUR OBJECTIONS, RIGHT?

YOON AND LEE, TOO... WE'LL ALL FOLLOW THROUGH.
I...
I DID REFUSE.
EXCUSE ME...
...BUT CAN'T WE CONSIDER UNIONIZATION HERE?
UNION-IZATION?

DOES OUR COMPANY EVEN HAVE A UNION?
YEAH. THE JUNGSAN BRANCH HAS ONE.
...
THAT... COULD THAT WORK?
MAYBE. AT MY PREVIOUS COMPANY, EMPLOYEES WEREN'T MOVED TO FULL-TIME EVEN AFTER A YEAR...
...SO DISCONTENT AMONG THEM WAS HIGH.
WE MADE PLANS WITH THE STORE MANAGER'S SECRETARY TO "LEAK" INFORMATION ABOUT THE EMPLOYEES FORMING A UNION.
WHAT? A LABOR UNION?
THEY IMMEDIATELY CONVERTED US TO FULL-TIME.
THAT WAS BACK WHEN THE FRENCH WERE NAIVE ABOUT BUSINESS IN KOREA.
WOULD IT WORK NOW?
WOULDN'T IT CARRY WEIGHT FOR US, AS MANAGERS, TO JOIN?

HMM...
I THINK IT'S WORTH A SHOT.
I'LL TAKE CARE OF GETTING THE PAPERWORK TOGETHER. WE CAN MEET HERE TOMORROW TO FILL IT OUT TOGETHER.
LET'S DO IT!
THEY CAN'T FIRE ALL OF US, RIGHT?

SO... WE BEGIN OUR STRUGGLE HERE, HUH?
WHAT CAN'T WE DO WITH A GOOD MINDSET? COME ON. LET'S FIGHT!
FRESH FOODS DEPARTMENT!
LET'S FIGHT!
SO, WE'RE MEETING AFTER WORK TOMORROW?
YES!
MR. LEE, MAKE SURE YOU BRING THE REGISTRATION FORM!
YOU CAN COUNT ON ME.

푸르미 노동조합
FOURMIS LABOR UNION
MEMBER LOGIN
아이디
비밀번호
로그인
회원가입
AH... THERE IT IS.

I... MY WIFE SAID SHE'D DIVORCE ME IF I JOINED A UNION...
I ASKED MY OLD BOSS FOR HIS ADVICE, AND HE SAID IT'S A BAD IDEA...
ABSENT.
WELL... I CAN'T DO IT WITHOUT EVERYBODY ELSE GOING IN.
WELL... AND YOU, MR. LEE...?
I FAXED THE REGISTRATION FORM THIS MORNING.
풉
PFFTU

SHOULD I RUN AWAY AGAIN?
I ALREADY ESCAPED AND FOUND MYSELF HERE.
IF I RUN AGAIN, WHERE COULD I GO?
WILL THERE EVER BE A PLACE I DON'T WANT TO ESCAPE?
Fourmis

WHAT ABOUT A COUPLE OF HOURS?
IF IT'S NOT POSSIBLE TO STAY FOR A WHOLE NIGHT, WOULD A COUPLE OF HOURS BE OKAY? "NEAR THE COMPANY," BUT WITHIN WHAT DISTANCE, EXACTLY?
4. The company can punish those who stay overnight in grou
company premises or those who disseminate company docur
without authorization.
5. The company reserves the right to take additional measur
event
cation of defamatory documents.
THIS IS THE PROPOSAL YOU'RE SUBMITTING?
DO YOU HAVE ANY REAL INTENTION TO NEGOTIATE HERE?
YOU BASTARDS! YOU THINK I DON'T KNOW THAT YOU ALL GATHERED AT A HOTEL...
...TO INVESTIGATE MY BACKGROUND AND REPORT ME TO THE TAX OFFICE?!

SIR, HAVE YOU FORGOTTEN RESPECTFUL FORMS OF ADDRESS? WE'RE IN THE MIDDLE OF A NEGOTIATION!
THIS DAMN-- *DON'T YOU POINT AT ME!*
MR. CHOI, THIS GUY ISN'T EVEN A COMPANY EMPLOYEE, SO WHAT'S HE DOING HERE? GET RID OF HIM!
WE WERE NOTIFIED AHEAD OF TIME THAT HE'D BE NEGOTIATING ON BEHALF OF THE UNION. IT'S LEGITIMATE.
AND I'M NOT AN EMPLOYEE HERE, EITHER.
WELL, WHAT KIND OF LEGAL SYSTEM ARE WE RUNNING UNDER?!
SOME GUY I'VE NEVER SEEN BEFORE ARRIVES TO STEAL MY ASSETS, AND I'M JUST SUPPOSED TO SIT STILL AND TAKE IT?!

A COLLECTIVE AGREEMENT IS AN AGREEMENT ON WORKING CONDITIONS. YOU CANNOT IMPOSE A CONTRACT WHERE RESTRICTIONS ON PERSONAL FREEDOM ARE APPLIED!
결투쟁
PRESENTING THIS RIDICULOUS NEGOTIATION PLAN SEEMS LIKE INTENTIONAL NEGLIGENCE! SHOULD I FILE A COMPLAINT?
RIDICULOUS?!
DO YOU KNOW HOW MUCH THE NATIONAL TAX SERVICE RIPPED ME OFF?!
IF YOUR PROPOSALS MAKE SENSE, HERE'S MY COUNTER-PROPOSAL...
"CEO IL-HO JANG CAN'T WATCH PORN FROM NOW ON!" HOW'S THAT?!
ARE YOU IMPLYING THAT OUR CEO WATCHES PORN VIDEOS?!!
WHY'D HE OBTAIN SO MANY FROM THE GENERAL AFFAIRS MANAGER IF HE WASN'T GOING TO WATCH THEM?

IL-HO, WHAT THE HELL IS THIS GUY TALKING ABOUT?
IT LOOKS LIKE YOUR BELOVED SON, WHO YOU APPOINTED CEO, IS FINALLY BEHAVING LIKE A MAN. LOVELY...
DIRECTOR JANG, IS THAT ANY WAY TO TALK ABOUT YOUR OLDER BROTHER?!
...
I'LL TREAT HIM LIKE A BIG BROTHER WHEN HE STARTS ACTING LIKE ONE!
YOU SHOULD HAVE NAMED ME CEO! WHY DID A UNION FORM? A UNION!
IF I HAD APPOINTED YOU, WOULD THE COMPANY HAVE SURVIVED? YOU'D HAVE GIVEN THE OFFICE TO YOUR HUSBAND!!
단결 투쟁
단결 투쟁
ARE YOU NOT GOING TO NEGOTIATE? SHOULD WE JUST GO ON STRIKE?
EH?
AH, YES... WE'LL NEGOTIATE.

WOW, A FORMIDABLE FOE... TRULY FORMIDABLE.
TOLD YOU SO. OUR COMPANY'S A TOTAL JOKE.
WANT TO HAVE LUNCH WITH US?
I HAVE TO TAKE CARE OF SOME THINGS.
THEN WE'LL HEAD OUT. THANKS AGAIN FOR YOUR HARD WORK.
SURE THING.
PSSHHH
HELLO?
HEY! COMPANY MAN!!
CAN YOU STOP CALLING ME THAT?
I ALSO REPRESENT THE UNION SIDE OF THINGS, YOU KNOW.
I REMIND YOU THAT IT'S THANKS TO ME THAT YOU HAVE A JOB, SO MAKE SURE YOU DO IT WELL!

WHY DON'T YOU EDUCATE YOUR CLIENTS BEFORE TURNING THEM LOOSE?
HOW AM I SUPPOSED TO NEGOTIATE WITH 'EM IF THEY DON'T UNDERSTAND THE BASIC IDEA?
DO YOU WANT TO TRY GIVING THAT OLD MAN A LAW LESSON?
I'D BE WILLING TO PAY FOR THAT.
...
YOU'RE WORKING HARD, ATTORNEY CHOI!
KEEP IT UP!
YOU BET! SEE YOU AT THE NEXT NEGOTIATION.

* RESTAURANT SPECIALIZING IN AFFORDABLE MEALS FOR WORKERS

** ABOUT $427 USD AT CURRENT CONVERSTION RATE (2024)

RUSTLE
SWISH

PLEASE... PLEASE TAKE THIS!
MR. JANG...
WHAT'S THIS?
IT'S A DOWN PAYMENT.
I'D LIKE TO HAVE YOU ON AS THE LABOR DIRECTOR OF OUR COMPANY.
YOU HAVE A LOT OF HIGH-LEVEL POSITIONS FOR A SMALLER COMPANY... HOW MUCH?
WOW. THE CHAIRMAN'S POCKETS AREN'T VERY DEEP, HUH?
PLEASE ACCEPT IT.
IS YOUR DADDY GONNA SCOLD YOU IF YOU COME BACK WITH IT?
...

HERE. TAKE IT BACK.
UH... BUT YOU SHOULDN'T...
LET ME GIVE YOU SOMETHING INSTEAD.
척
FLIP!

TA-DA!
MR. IL-HO JANG ATTEMPTED TO BRIBE THE OPPOSING PARTY'S NEGOTIATOR, RIGHT?
NOW YOU'RE *REALLY* LOOKING AT CHARGES FOR UNFAIR LABOR PRACTICES.
YOU'RE SCARED OF THE CHAIRMAN, HUH?
WHO DO YOU THINK'S SCARIER, THE CHAIRMAN OR THE PROSECUTOR?
IF YOU DON'T WANT TO MEET THE PROSECUTOR, PLEASE NEGOTIATE HONESTLY.

Fourmis
SIR, YOU CAN'T DISTRIBUTE THESE HERE!
THIS IS THE SIDEWALK. YOU OWN THE SIDEWALK?
COULD YOU SPEAK TO ME WITH MORE RESPECT?
IF I SPEAK RESPECTFULLY, WON'T YOU STILL SEND ME AWAY?
EVEN IF I'M POLITE, YOU'LL STILL MAKE ME LEAVE, RIGHT?
WELL... YES...

IMAGINE AN OLD MAN LIKE ME LOWERING HIS HEAD FOR SOMEONE LIKE YOU!
WOULDN'T YOU FEEL GUILTY SHOOING SOMEONE LIKE THAT AWAY?
I ACT LIKE THIS TO KEEP YOU MORALLY COMFORTABLE!
WHAT ARE YOU...?
HEY THERE, PRETTY MISS. WHILE YOU'RE LAUGHING, TAKE ONE OF THESE.
CLEANING AND MEETING TIMES COUNT AS WORKING HOURS. DID YOU KNOW THAT?
THIS GUY REALLY... LOOK, IF YOU WANT TO DISTRIBUTE TRASH, GO ELSEWHERE!
Fourn
TRASH?! THESE ARE BUSINESS CARDS! I'M MAKING A LIVING HERE!

Fourmis

HOW MANY TIMES HAVE I TOLD YOU NOT TO WEAR SUCH HEAVY MAKEUP?
BUT...IT'S THE SAME AS YESTERDAY, AND--
EXACTLY. YOU KEEP MAKING THE SAME MISTAKE!
YOU THINK THIS IS ACCEPTABLE? WELL, YOU'RE WRONG!
IF YOU'RE GOING TO KEEP MESSING UP, YOU MIGHT AS WELL QUIT!
THESE KINDS OF SCENES ARE COMMON. NOTHING SPECIAL.
BUT NOW THEY AVOID MY EYES.
THE PURPOSE OF THEIR ACTIONS HAS SHIFTED.

투
CLACK
각
THIS IS STILL OUT ON THE FLOOR THIS LATE IN THE MORNING?!
WHO DID THIS DISPLAY?
YOU? AND DID YOU CLEAN THEM?
YES... OF COURSE I DID...
IF YOU DID IT, SHOULDN'T IT BE MORE EVIDENT?
DON'T YOU WANT THIS JOB?
IF YOU DON'T, THEN DON'T PRETEND TO DO IT!
THE STREETS ARE FULL OF PEOPLE READY TO REPLACE YOU!
THEY WERE IMPLEMENTING ALL MEANS AND METHODS.
MR. JEONG, LET'S DISCUSS THIS LATER.

LATER? AND WHEN WILL THAT BE?
IT'S ALMOST OPENING TIME NOW, SO...
I'M HANDLING THIS IN THE FIRST PLACE BECAUSE YOU HAVEN'T PROPERLY MANAGED YOUR TEAM FOR OPENING!
AND WHY ARE YOU, AS A MANAGER, WEARING A FLOOR STAFF APRON?!
DO YOU UNDERSTAND YOUR OWN ROLE?
IT'S A MANAGER'S JOB TO INSTRUCT OTHERS!

I FEEL LIKE A RABBIT WHO'S SUDDENLY JUMPED INTO THE ROAD.
WELL, CALLING MYSELF A RABBIT HURTS MY PRIDE, SO LET'S USE A DEER INSTEAD.
HIS HANDS HESITATE ON THE WHEEL FOR A MOMENT, BUT THEN HE REALIZES THAT HE'S NOT IN CONTROL OF THE STEERING OR THE BRAKES.
THE ONLY THING HE CAN DO IS HONK THE HORN AS HE ADVANCES.
...
...
"MOVE! PLEASE MOVE!"
"WHY ARE YOU IN MY WAY? EVERYONE ELSE HAS RUN AWAY, SO WHY ARE YOU STANDING HERE?!"
...
...
I WISH I COULD MOVE. I'M GOING CRAZY STANDING HERE LIKE THIS.

YOU OKAY, HON?
WHY'S MR. JEONG ACTING LIKE THIS?
HE'S UPSET WITH MANAGER LEE.
THAT'S NOT REALLY SURPRISING, IS IT?
IF YOU'RE MAD AT SOMEONE, DIRECT IT AT THAT PERSON...
YEAH, FOR SURE...
THAT WAS AWFUL.
WE CAN GET DRINKS LATER...
THERE'S NO WINNING WITH THOSE LADIES...
MAN...

OH? MR. LEE...
WE'RE ON OUR WAY BACK IN.
HEY, BY THE WAY...
ARE YOU GOING TO WITHDRAW FROM THE UNION?
AH, WELL... I'M ALONE, IN ANY CASE...
THEY NEVER REACHED OUT TO ME.
I UNDERSTAND. WISE DECISION.
STAY STRONG.
STAY STRONG? STAY STRONG AND WHAT?
STAY STRONG AND HARASS YOUR EMPLOYEES?

VRRRRR
VRRRRR
HELLO?
IS THIS MR. SOO-IN LEE?
YES, IT IS.
THIS IS THE FOURMIS LABOR UNION.
OH...
YES!
YOU SENT US A REGISTRATION FORM, RIGHT?
YES!
THERE'S A MEETING FOR UNION MEMBERS OF THE ILDONG BRANCH TONIGHT.
I'M SORRY FOR THE LATE NOTICE, BUT...
AH, YES. I CAN BE THERE!
THIS EVENING?
YES.

HEADBAND SLOGAN: "FIGHT UNITED!"

WE'RE MEETING AT A RESTAURANT ACROSS FROM THE ILDONG BRANCH.
IN ADDITION TO YOU, SEVERAL MORE MEMBERS WILL BE COMING.
SO, I'M NOT ALONE AFTER ALL?
YES...
ALRIGHT. I UNDERSTAND.
W-WOW, IT'S... OUR MANAGER...?!
HUH? MR. LEE... SIR...
MISSUS...
...JEONG-MI KIM AND YEONG-SIL HAN ARE HERE.

OH! YOU ALL KNOW EACH OTHER?
AH, YES... THESE ARE EMPLOYEES OF MY DEPARTMENT.
WOW, AMAZING! THESE LADIES SIGNED UP ABOUT THREE MONTHS AGO!
WHAT A COINCIDENCE THAT YOU ALL UNWITTINGLY JOINED TOGETHER.
ALLOW ME TO INTRODUCE MYSELF. I'M GYEONG-MI IN, HEAD OF THE FOURMIS UNION.
I'M JONG-HAK YOO, UNION CHAIRMAN.
I'M SOO-IN LEE.
LET'S SIT DOWN.
I THOUGHT I HEARD YOUR MANAGER WAS SOME KIND OF CRAZY PSYCHOPATH?
PSYCHO...PATH...?
AGH!
UGH!
BUT... I GUESS THAT ASSESSMENT ISN'T UNANIMOUS...
...AND HE'S NOT REALLY CRAZY.

WELL, IT'S... MR. LEE ALWAYS FAVORS EMPLOYEES FROM PARTNER COMPANIES.
CRAZY... PSYCHOPATH...
WE THOUGHT HE MEANT TO UNDERMINE US...
RIGHT. AND OUR PREVIOUS MANAGER WOULD EVEN GO OUT TO KARAOKE WITH US, BUT MR. LEE'S SO COLD...
CRAZY...
...PSYCHO-PATH...
THAT'S WHY WE JOINED THE UNION.
I... I GUESS I WAS DOING MY JOB WELL EVEN WITHOUT JEONG TELLING ME WHAT TO DO.
토종 순대국
IN A SITUATION LIKE THIS, THERE'S NOT MUCH THE UNION CAN DO RIGHT NOW...
...SINCE THERE'S NO PHYSICAL EVIDENCE.

I DON'T KNOW IF YOU'RE AWARE, BUT WE'VE BEEN AT THIS FOR THREE YEARS AND HAVE ONLY JUST BEGUN NEGOTIATIONS.
WE DON'T CURRENTLY HAVE THE STRENGTH TO DO MUCH.
WE SHOULD FIRST FOCUS ON INCREASING THE NUMBER OF UNION MEMBERS TO BUILD UP OUR BARGAINING POWER.
HOW MANY UNION MEMBERS ARE THERE NOW?
THERE WERE 300, BUT AFTER THREE YEARS... NOW THERE'S ONLY 52 MEMBERS...
WE'RE A SMALL UNION THAT'S JUST STARTING ITS FIRST NEGOTIATIONS, BUT IF YOU ALL HELP...

THE CLUMSY VIOLENCE THAT WAS ONCE CARRIED OUT RELUCTANTLY IS NOW ROUTINE.
THOSE WHO AVOIDED EYE CONTACT WITH ME NO LONGER AVOID IT, NOR DO THEY HIDE THEIR EXPRESSIONS OF CONTEMPT, BOREDOM, AND ANNOYANCE.
IT'S THE SAME LOOK YOU SET ON AN UNINVITED GUEST WHO SHAMELESSLY REFUSES TO LEAVE.
IT'S A FAMILIAR LOOK, BUT IT'S HARD TO GET USED TO.

AFTER SEVERAL DAYS OF TYRANNY...
...IT WAS AS IF THE EMPLOYEES, ONCE RELAXED AND SKILLFUL SERGEANTS...
...RETURNED TO BE BEING NEWLY TRANSFERRED PRIVATES.

ALL NEW RECRUITS HAD THAT CHARACTERISTIC, FRIGHTENED EXPRESSION.
THERE WAS AN EXCESSIVENESS IN THE VIOLENCE OF THEIR SENIORS THAT COULDN'T BE EXPLAINED AWAY BY SAYING IT WAS SIMPLY TO MAINTAIN DISCIPLINE.
PERHAPS THAT EXPRESSION, THAT DISPLAY OF WEAKNESS, WORKED TO TRIGGER THEIR HATRED.
AND THEY CAN BECOME TRULY CRUEL...
...TO THOSE THEY HATE.

THAT BASTARD...
ALL DAY LONG...
HOW CAN HE... HE'S YOUNGER THAN MY YOUNGEST NEPHEW!
...OUT OF SIGHT FROM THE MANAGERS...
...
ARE YOU ALRIGHT, DEAR?
SOB...
SOB...
...EMPLOYEES WERE HIDDEN AWAY SOBBING.
SALES AREA ENTRANCE
SALES AREA ENTRANCE

WELCOME...
...TO FOURMIS!

IS THERE ENOUGH BROCCOLI OUT CURRENTLY?
I THINK WE'RE FINE UNTIL THE AFTERNOON.
I'LL CHECK WITH THE WAREHOUSE ABOUT PREPPING IT FOR THEN.
WE HAVE THE SAME PRODUCTS AND THE SAME PROMOTIONS, SO WHY ARE SALES DROPPING...?
GOOD MORNING.
HEY, KANG-MIN...

YES, BOSS?
AFTER OPENING, GO TO THE NEIGHBORING BRANCH...
SURE!
...AND TAKE PHOTOS OF THE FRUIT AND VEGETABLE DISPLAYS TO SHOW MR. YOON.
EXCUSE ME, BUT... SHOULDN'T THAT BE THE MANAGER'S JOB? HE'S RIGHT THERE.
YOU'VE WORKED HERE LONG ENOUGH. LET'S NOT MAKE DISTINCTIONS. JUST GO.
YES, SIR...
SORRY, MR. LEE...
DON'T WORRY ABOUT IT. GO ON.

MR. LEE, AREN'T YOU GOING TO THE MEETING?
AH, YES... I JUST HAVE TO PULL UP MY MEETING MATERIALS...
User name
f22
Login failed
OK

MR. KIM...
YES, MR. LEE?
I CAN'T SEEM TO ACCESS THE INTRANET.
OH, REALLY? WHAT'S YOUR I.D.?
F22.
OH? THAT'S **YOUR** I.D.?
I WAS TOLD TO BLOCK IT...
WHO... TOLD YOU THAT?
...
UH... WELL...
I DON'T THINK I SHOULD DIVULGE THAT...

FORGIVE ME FOR BEING LATE.
DON'T BOTHER SITTING DOWN.
THE MEETING'S OVER.
DID YOU TRY TO COME EMPTY-HANDED, TOO?
DON'T YOU HAVE ANY MEETING MATERIALS?
WELL, I COULDN'T...
THE INTRANET...

WHAT'S WRONG WITH THE INTRANET? ISN'T IT WORKING JUST FINE?
LET'S GO EAT.
WE DRANK LAST NIGHT, SO LET'S HAVE SOMETHING REFRESHING TODAY.
THERE WAS A COMPANY DINNER YESTERDAY?
AH, YEAH...
DIDN'T I TELL YOU?
SHIN! AREN'T YOU COMING?
OH. YES...

NO WAY...
WAS HE SMILING?
HEY, LEE, LET'S GO EAT.
HUH? WEREN'T YOU GOING WITH THEM?
I TOLD THEM I WAS BUSY.
EVEN KIDS AREN'T THAT CHILDISH... LET'S GO.

YOU EVER TRIED BOXING?
WHAT?
BOXING. **BOXING.**
OH. NO.
HEY, MAN, WANNA SPAR?
YOU'VE BEEN COMING HERE FOR ABOUT THREE MONTHS, RIGHT?
GIVE IT A SHOT.
WHEN YOU FIRST GET IN THE RING, YOU DON'T KNOW WHAT TO DO WITH YOURSELF.
ALL YOU CAN DO IS KEEP YOUR GUARD UP, KEEP YOUR HEAD DOWN...
...AND TRY TO DODGE YOUR OPPONENT'S ATTACKS.
IT SEEMS STUPID TO SAY, BUT THAT LACK OF MOVEMENT CAN HURT YOUR PRIDE.

IT'S NATURAL FOR A BEGINNER TO GET HIT.
NO ONE'S LAUGHING AT YOU FOR THAT, BUT YOU CAN'T HELP BUT GET ANGRY ABOUT IT.
AND THEN YOU WIND UP DOING SOMETHING YOU SHOULDN'T.
YOU HIT BACK.
AND YOU KNOW WHAT THAT JAB MEANS?
"I HAVE FISTS, TOO."

WHO DOESN'T KNOW YOU HAVE FISTS?
YOU KNOW IT, I KNOW IT, THE WHOLE WORLD KNOWS IT.
SO SHOWING THEM DOESN'T PROVE ANY UNKNOWNS...
...BUT YOU STILL WANNA DO IT.
AND THAT ONE GESTURE'S GOING TO EARN YOU ALL THE OTHER HITS YOU COULD'VE AVOIDED.
AFTER THAT, YOU THINK... MAYBE YOU WON'T GET INTO THE RING THE NEXT DAY, RIGHT?
BUT YOU WILL. YOU KNOW WHY?

NO IDEA.
AT NIGHT, WHEN YOU CLOSE YOUR EYES, ALL THE HITS YOU TOOK COME BACK.
IT FEELS UNFAIR, EMBARRASSING...
THEN, THAT ONE SHOT YOU MANAGED TO GET IN...
...COMES THROUGH CRYSTAL-CLEAR.
THAT HIT THAT BARELY GRAZED YOUR OPPONENT...
...TRANSFORMS ITSELF INTO A FANTASTIC BLOW.
JUST LIKE THAT, EVEN IF YOU DON'T WIN, YOU DON'T COMPLETELY LOSE.
IT'S LIKE AN ILLUSION.
THE NEXT DAY, YOU GET INTO THE RING AGAIN, AND YOU GET KICKED AROUND SOME MORE. HEH, HEH.
YOU SEE WHAT I'M SAYING?

YEAH...
STILL, YOU HAVE TO KEEP AT IT TO IMPROVE YOUR SKILLS...
HUH?
UH...
IN BOXING, I MEAN.
HEY, HEY! YOU'RE GONNA GET HURT.
STOP AND COME DOWN!

IN THE RING, THERE'S ALWAYS SOMEONE WILLING TO HELP YOU.
THERE'S NO SUCH THING HERE.

EVEN IF YOU DIE, YOU HAVE TO GO OUT ALONE.
NO ONE EVEN COMES TO CLEAN IT UP.

WHEN'S THE LAST TIME YOU ORGANIZED YOUR STOCK?
I CAN'T TELL IF YOU HAVE A WAREHOUSE OR A LANDFILL BACK THERE.
YOU KNOW JEONG'S GOT SOME KIND OF INFERIORITY COMPLEX TOWARDS YOU, RIGHT?
WHAT? TOWARDS ME?
DO YOU REALLY NOT KNOW? OR ARE YOU JUST PLAYING DUMB?
YOU WERE HIRED FROM OUTSIDE THE COMPANY AND HAVE A GOOD TRACK RECORD. IT'S CLEAR CORPORATE HAS A PLAN FOR YOU.

IT'S A MIRACLE
EONG'S RISEN TO HIS POSITION.
HE CAN'T EVEN TALK TO THE STORE MANAGER IF YOU'RE NOT THERE TO TRANSLATE.
CAN YOU IMAGINE HOW FRUSTRATING THAT MUST BE?
HIS BLUSTER IS ALL INSECURITY, TO TRY AND BE HEARD. I ALMOST PITY HIM.
IT'S CLEAR HE WOULDN'T ACT LIKE THIS IF IT WEREN'T FOR YOU.
I FIGURE YOU OUGHT TO JUST BEAR IT FOR NOW. SOON ENOUGH, YOU'LL ADVANCE WAY PAST HIM.
GUARD UP, HEAD DOWN.

I'M TIRED.
IT'S ALWAYS THE SAME BASIC ADVICE FROM PEOPLE PRETENDING TO BE WISE...
...DRESSED UP IN CLICHÉS LIKE IT'S SOME BRAND-NEW INSIGHT.
...
...
BUT, IN REALITY...
YES, I'LL DEAL WITH IT RIGHT AWAY.
...THE ANSWER'S ALWAYS FOUND IN THAT BASIC ADVICE.

MR. JEONG, THE STORE MANAGER'S COMING.
OH?

LEE, WHAT ARE YOU DOING? THE BOSS IS CALLING YOU.
HEY! MR. LEE!

MR. LEE, WHY DIDN'T YOU FOLLOW MY ORDERS?
YOU ORDERED ME TO RE-ORGANIZE MY DEPARTMENT. BULLYING THE EMPLOYEES IS NOT RE-ORGANIZATION.

NO, NO, NO...
I MAKE THE DECISIONS. YOU JUST FOLLOW ORDERS.
THE CUSTOMERS CAN SEE US. THIS PROBABLY DOESN'T LOOK GOOD.
SMILE, MR. LEE. THEN WE'LL SEEM LIKE CHEERFUL CO-WORKERS.
YOU SHOULD ALWAYS SMILE HERE. THAT'S PART OF YOUR JOB.
I HEARD SOME BAD NEWS.
MR. LEE, DID YOU JOIN THE UNION?
DO YOU WANT TO TURN AGAINST ME? YOU PICKED THE WRONG PERSON.

I'M VERY TOUGH.
LET ME SHOW YOU.
GATHER YOUR DEPARTMENT.
I'VE MADE AN IMPORTANT DECISION.
THERE WILL BE NO PROMOTIONS...
MR. LEE, TRANSLATE!

FOR YOU, THERE WILL BE NO PROMOTIONS...
...NOR WILL THERE BE ANY SALARY RAISES OR TRANSFERS TO A DIFFERENT BRANCH.
YOU WILL NOT BE PROMOTED FURTHER.
THERE WILL BE NO WAGE INCREASES OR TRANSFERS TO ANOTHER STORE.
INSTEAD, YOU WILL GO THROUGH HELL, WORKING UNDER ME FOR ALL ETERNITY.
YOU WILL SUFFER UNDER ME FOREVER.
WHY?
WHY?
BECAUSE OF YOUR MANAGER, MR. LEE.

BE...
BECAUSE...
...OF YOUR MANAGER...
...SOO-IN LEE.

GOOD JOB.

AH, MR. KIM...
WHAT NOW?
WHAT SHOULD I DO NOW?

I FEEL LIKE SHIT...
...BUT I'M NOT CONFUSED ANYMORE.

I'M ALREADY DEAD...
...AND I HAVE NO INTENTION OF CLEANING IT UP BY MYSELF.

I CHALLENGE YOU
TO GET RID OF ME.

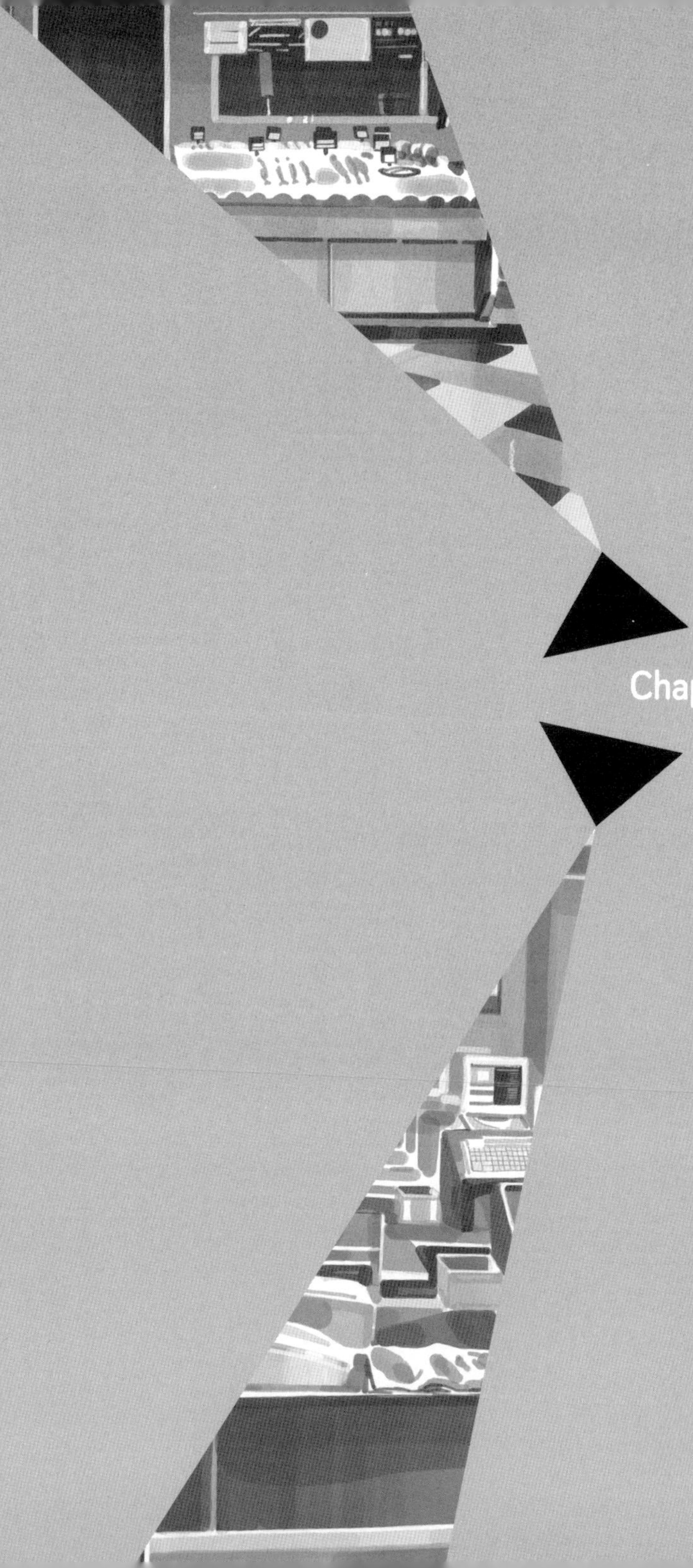

Chapter 2

IT DOESN'T LOOK VERY STABLE...
HEY, MR. PARK, SHOULDN'T WE SECURE THESE?
WE DON'T HAVE TIME FOR THAT. GET UP THERE AND HOLD 'EM.
WHAT? BUT WHAT IF I FALL?
C'MON, WE'RE NOT GOING THAT FAR...
BUT... IT'D BE BETTER TO JUST GET A TARP OVER IT OR MAKE ANOTHER TRIP...

ANOTHER TRIP?
YOU GONNA PAY FOR THE GAS?
...
부
우
우
우
VROOOM

덜컹
THUD
OH...
OH...!
AAH!
MR. PARK!
ST--
STOP!

THANK GOODNESS THE TRUCK WAS GOING SLOW AND I HAD THE BAGS TO BREAK MY FALL...
IF IT WEREN'T FOR THAT, I'D HAVE BEEN IN REAL TROUBLE.
I SPENT A LITTLE WHILE IN THE HOSPITAL, AND MY EXPENSES WERE PAID BY THE COMPANY...
...BUT I STILL HAVEN'T COMPLETELY RECOVERED.
WHY ARE YOU SADDLING ME WITH THAT GEEZER? EVEN IF I RUN AROUND ALL NIGHT, I WON'T GET ANYTHING DONE!
LOOK, IT'S JUST FOR A FEW DAYS. CONSIDER THE COMPANY'S SITUATION.
BEING A SANITATION MAN'S MUCH HARDER THAN IT SEEMS.
I GO TO WORK AFTER DINNER AND DON'T GET TO EAT AGAIN UNTIL NEXT DAY'S LUNCH. PLUS, I'M ON MY FEET FOR THE WHOLE THING.
EVEN YOUNG GUYS COMPLAIN ABOUT THE PAIN.
BUT I'M OLD AND WEAK, SO I'VE JUST BECOME A BURDEN...
I CAN'T WORK PROPERLY, SO I FEEL GUILTY ABOUT RECEIVING MY SALARY...
...AND I KNOW THE COMPANY WANTS ME GONE...

ARE YOU IN A POSITION TO WORRY ABOUT OTHERS?
DO YOU HAVE ANY SAVINGS?
AFRAID NOT.
ANY PROPERTY OR LAND?
OH MY, NO...
KIDS WILLING TO HELP YOU OUT?
THEY'RE CAUGHT UP IN THEIR OWN LIVES...
SO WHAT ARE YOU GOING TO DO IF YOU GET FIRED?
YOU HAVE TO EARN A LIVING WITH YOUR OWN BODY, RIGHT?
BUT YOUR BODY IS BROKEN...
...SO YOU'RE SCREWED NOW.
WHAT DO YOU THINK YOU'LL ACHIEVE BY PUTTING ON A NICE FACE FOR THEM?
...

HAS ANYONE BEEN DISMISSED SINCE YOUR ACCIDENT?
I DON'T THINK SO... WHY?
YOU'LL NEED A WITNESS TO FILE FOR WORKERS' COMPENSATION...
...BUT IT'S UNLIKELY THAT SOMEONE STILL WITH THE COMPANY WILL HELP.
I DID HEAR THAT WORKERS' COMP WAS AN OPTION, THAT I MIGHT BE ABLE TO GET A MONTHLY AMOUNT, BUT WHEN I ASKED ABOUT IT...
INDUSTRIAL ACCIDENT? DID SOMEONE THROW YOU UP THERE? YOU DIDN'T CLIMB UP YOURSELF?
THE COMPANY'S ALREADY PAID YOUR MEDICAL BILLS, SO YOU CAN'T FILE FOR COMPENSATION.
THEY'RE LYING. THEY DON'T WANT TO GET AUDITED BY THE DEPARTMENT OF LABOR AND HAVE THEIR INSURANCE RATES GO UP.
REGARDLESS OF WHAT YOUR COMPANY SAYS, YOU CAN SUBMIT A MEDICAL TREATMENT APPLICATION TO THE KOREA WORKERS' COMPENSATION AND WELFARE SERVICE.

SO, YOU ABSOLUTELY NEED TO FIND A WITNESS.
IF YOU DON'T FIND ONE, YOU'RE DONE FOR. KEEP THAT IN MIND.
그르르르르르...
RATTLE...
탁
TAP
탁
TAP
탁
TAP
UGH...
AAH...
그르르르르르르
RATTLE...
WOW, YOU'RE REALLY MOVING AT A CRAWL. CRAWL FASTER.

SHIFT'S ALMOST OVER. HOW ARE WE SUPPOSED TO FINISH OUR ROUTE AT THIS RATE?
SORRY... I'M NOT FEELING WELL...
IF YOU'RE NOT ABLE TO WORK, YOU SHOULD STAY HOME. YOU'RE JUST SLOWING US DOWN.
CLANG
HEY, MR. KIM...
WHAT?
YOU KNOW THAT ACCIDENT I HAD THE OTHER DAY?
WHAT ABOUT IT?
CAN YOU WRITE A WITNESS STATEMENT FOR ME?
THAT WAY, I CAN RECEIVE COMPENSATION.

LEAVE ME OUT OF IT.
SOME PEOPLE HAVE NO SHAME...
WHAT ARE YOU DOING? BACK TO WORK.
AH... HELLO. IT'S HONG.
CAN I REALLY NOT FILE A CLAIM WITHOUT A WITNESS?
WHY? NOBODY'S STEPPED UP?
THE COMPANY'S A TIGHT SHIP. THEY'VE COMPLETELY SHUT ME DOWN.
DON'T GIVE UP. YOU SHOULD LET ME MEET WITH A FEW OF THEM!
IT'S FINE. I DON'T WANT ANYONE TO RISK LOSING THEIR JOB BECAUSE OF ME...
MR. HONG! WAIT FOR ME THERE. I'M COMING!
NO... I DON'T WANT TO BE A BOTHER.

푸 득
FLAP
푸 드 득
FLAP
SQUEAK SQUEAK
OH, YIKES!

HEH. I GUESS RATS AREN'T IN BED AT THIS HOUR.
HUH? IT'S MR. GU.
WHAT'RE YOU DOING HERE?
ARE YOU ALLOWED HERE...?
I'M NOT HERE FOR YOU. WHERE'S THE WASTE MANAGEMENT COMPANY?
HEYYY! WHAT'S UP, FELLAS?

EH?
THERE YOU ARE, MR. HONG.
I... I TOLD YOU NOT TO WORRY ABOUT IT ANYMORE, SO...
DO I SEEM WORRIED?
GENTLEMEN.
A MOMENT OF YOUR TIME, PLEASE.
MR. JONG-GAP HONG HERE IS A GOOD FRIEND OF MINE...
I'M SURE YOU ALL KNOW HE WAS SUBJECT TO AN ACCIDENT WHILE ON DUTY NOT LONG AGO.
YOU KNOW...
WELL, YOU KNOW ALL ABOUT IT, DON'T YOU?
YOU FEEL YOU CAN'T SPEAK UP, BUT THAT'S NOT SITTING WELL WITH YOUR CONSCIENCE, RIGHT?
THOSE WHO SUFFER INDUSTRIAL ACCIDENTS ARE ENTITLED TO TREATMENT WHILE ADDITIONALLY RECEIVING 70 PERCENT OF THEIR WAGES.

BUT THE FACT IS THAT ONE NEEDS A WITNESS TO FILE A COMPENSATION CLAIM.
IS IT RIGHT THAT A WORKER WHOSE BODY'S BEEN HARMED SIMPLY STARVE TO DEATH?
HERE'S MY BUSINESS CARD. HANG ON TO IT.
IF YOU FIND YOU CAN'T SLEEP AT NIGHT, DON'T HESITATE TO CALL ME.
EXCUSE ME, BUT... IF YOU'RE A WITNESS, WON'T THE COMPANY FIND OUT?
YEP.
THAT'S WHY I'M APPEALING TO YOUR CONSCIENCE.
IF YOU'RE FIRED FOR THIS, I WILL HELP GET YOU REINSTATED, FREE OF CHARGE.
IF NOT BY LAW, THEN BY FORCE.
I KNOW IT'S HARD TO MAKE A LIVING.
STILL, YOU NEVER KNOW WHO'S GETTING HURT NEXT, RIGHT?
THE BEST THING'S FOR US TO ALL HELP EACH OTHER.
HEY! THIS GUY...!
I KNOW YOU! YOU'RE SOME KINDA COMMIE, RIGHT?
ISN'T YOUR "LABOR COUNSELING CENTER" A GATHERING PLACE FOR COMMUNISTS?

*HOTLINE FOR REPORTING CRIMES AGAINST NATIONAL SECURITY

YOU DON'T HAVE THE GUTS TO HELP A COWORKER WHO WAS INJURED ON THE JOB, BUT YOU HAVE NO SCRUPLES ABOUT KILLING ANOTHER HUMAN BEING.
I'M DONE WITH MY BUSINESS HERE. LET ME GO.
YOU... YOU RUNNING AWAY?
HUH? COME BACK HERE!
HEY! LET'S GO!
I'LL SHOW YOU, YOU BASTARD!
WELL, THEN... TAKE CARE AT WORK.

AND TAKE CARE OF EACH OTHER, ALRIGHT?
PLEASE REACH OUT TO ME.
IF YOU GRAB, SHAKE, AND SQUEEZE THE SHELL OF COWARDICE THAT SURROUNDS THESE SITUATIONS...
EVEN IF IT MEANS PUTTING THE SCREWS TO YOUR BOSS...
...I'LL MAKE SURE NO ONE HERE SUFFERS FOR IT.
...AT LEAST ONE PERSON WILL BREAK THROUGH.

HEY, BOSS, WHY'S MR. HONG WITH ME AGAIN?
I'M ALWAYS LATE WRAPPING UP WHEN I'M WITH HIM. WHY KEEP STICKING HIM WITH ME?
EXCUSE ME... I CAN TAKE MR. HONG IN MY TRUCK TODAY.
YOU VOLUNTEERING? ALRIGHT. GOOD TO SEE YOUNG PEOPLE STEPPING UP.
BUT DON'T DO HIS WORK FOR HIM, OKAY?
THE DRIVER AND COLLECTOR ARE TWO DISTINCT POSITIONS.
IF A DRIVER STARTS TOUCHING TRASH, THE ROLES WILL GET CONFUSED.
KEEPING THEM SEPARATE MAINTAINS COMPANY DISCIPLINE.
WELL, IT'S YOUR RESPONSIBILITY TODAY... BE CAREFUL WITH IT.
YOU'RE WITH ME.
AH, DONG-MAN...

I'M SURE AT LEAST ONE PERSON
WILL BREAK THROUGH THAT SHELL...

...DESPITE THE FEAR THAT THE NEXT STEP
MIGHT BE A CLIFF.

THEY'LL FIND THAT THEY CAN'T HELP THEMSELVES IN TAKING THAT STEP.

PIERCING THROUGH...

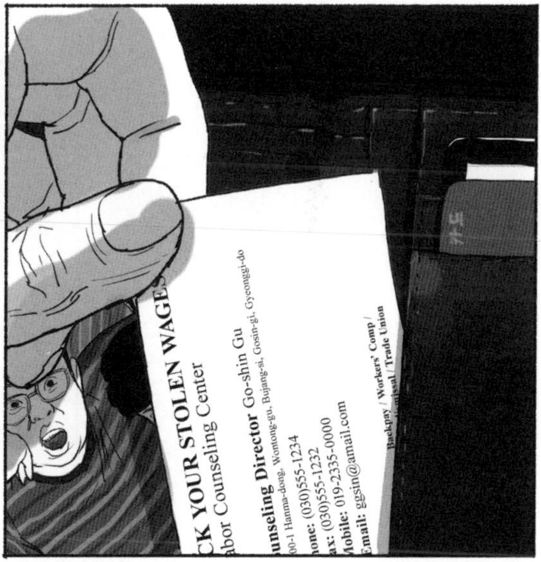

...AS IF THEY'D BECOME
AN AWL.

*BUSHIN LABOR COUNSELING CENTER

EXCUSE ME...
드르르륵
SLIIIIDE

벌나
져불
허벌나게
조져불자
T-SHIRT SLOGAN: "LET'S MESS SHIT UP"
허벌나
조져불
YOU HERE FOR A CONSULTATION?
HANG OUT FOR A MINUTE. WE'RE ALMOST DONE HERE.

ANYWAY, THE THREE LABOR RIGHTS ARE PROTECTED BY THE CONSTITUTION.
THESE ARE THE RIGHT TO ORGANIZE, THE RIGHT TO COLLECTIVE BARGAINING, AND THE RIGHT TO COLLECTIVE ACTION. BUT WHAT'S THAT MEAN?
WORKERS ARE ABLE TO GET TOGETHER AND NEGOTIATE WITH THE COMPANY, SETTING REQUIREMENTS...
...AND, IF THE COMPANY REFUSES NEGOTIATIONS, WORKERS CAN STRIKE IN PROTEST. THAT'S WHAT IT MEANS.
STRIKING IS AN INCREDIBLE TOOL. IF THERE'S A STRIKE, THERE'S NO WORK BEING DONE.
IF THERE'S NO WORK BEING DONE, THE COMPANY CAN'T DO BUSINESS.
EVEN IN THIS CAPITALIST SOCIETY, THE CONSTITUTION GUARANTEES THE RIGHT TO ASSEMBLE AND INTERVENE IN BUSINESS OPERATIONS.

*ABOUT $3,754 USD AT CURRENT CONVERSION RATE (2024)

*ABOUT $75,080 USD AT CURRENT CONVERSION RATE (2024)

*ABOUT $15,015 USD AT CURRENT CONVERSION RATE (2024)

**TAE-IL JEON WAS A GARMENT WORKER AND LABOR ACTIVIST WHO DIED VIA SELF-IMMOLATION IN 1970.

OPTIMISTIC TODAY, HUH?
UNIONS WERE FORMED EVEN BEFORE THESE LAWS WERE ADOPTED.
NOW, THOUGH, YOU DON'T GET DRAGGED AWAY AND TORTURED FOR GATHERING LIKE THIS TO STUDY LABOR LAW.
WE'VE COME A LONG WAY.
IN THE 1800S IN EUROPE, IT WAS ILLEGAL FOR TWO WORKERS TO EVEN MEET AT A BAR.
IN THE EARLY 1900S IN AMERICA, IT WAS POSSIBLE TO HIRE A SEVEN-YEAR-OLD FOR 14-HOUR SHIFTS.
THROUGHOUT HISTORY, ALL LABOR LAWS HAVE BEEN WRITTEN IN BLOOD.
WHOSE BLOOD?
PEOPLE LIKE YOU.
PEOPLE WHO CAN'T SIMPLY DO WHAT THEY'RE TOLD FOR THE PITTANCE AND POOR CONDITIONS THEY'RE GIVEN.

PEOPLE WHO CAN'T SIMPLY DO WHAT THEY'RE TOLD...
CONSULTATION GUY.
IS THAT YOUR FIRST TIME HEARING SOMETHING LIKE THAT?
AH. YES...
허벌나게
조저불자
THIS IS SOMETHING THEY SHOULD BE TEACHING IN SCHOOL.
IT DOESN'T MAKE SENSE TO HAVE TO LEARN IT AS AN ADULT.
IN GERMANY, ELEMENTARY STUDENTS HOLD MOCK LABOR NEGOTIATIONS SIX TIMES A YEAR.
THEY DRAFT DEMANDS, CREATE FLYERS, ORGANIZE PETITIONS, AND WRITE SPEECHES.
IN FRANCE, A THIRD OF THE HIGH SCHOOL SOCIAL STUDIES CURRICULUM IS DEVOTED TO NEGOTIATING STRATEGIES.
BECAUSE THIS IS TAUGHT IN SCHOOLS, JUDGES AND PROFESSORS IN THOSE COUNTRIES ALSO FORM UNIONS.

IN PLACES LIKE GERMANY AND SWEDEN, THERE ARE MILITARY UNIONS IN ADDITION TO POLICE AND FIREFIGHTER UNIONS.
BECAUSE OF THIS, CASES OF CORRUPTION, SEXUAL HARASSMENT, AND MYSTERIOUS DEATHS WITHIN THE MILITARY ARE MUCH RARER.
OUR COUNTRY HAS THE WORST WORKPLACE INJURY RATE AND THE HIGHEST WORKPLACE DEATH RATE, AND, WITHOUT A UNION, YOU CAN'T REPORT IT UNTIL YOU'RE DEAD.
EXCUSE ME...
FRENCH SOCIETY SEEMS FRIENDLY TOWARDS UNIONS...
CORRECT.
MY COMPANY IS A FRENCH COMPANY, AND THE BRANCH MANAGER IS ALSO FRENCH. WHY ARE THEY COMBATIVE TOWARDS OUR UNION?
BECAUSE THAT'S ACCEPTABLE HERE.

HERE, THEY AREN'T PUNISHED IF THEY BREAK THE LAW. THEY AREN'T CRITICIZED. THEY ONLY BENEFIT FROM IT.
WOULD ANYONE WITH A BRAIN SUFFER LOSSES BY OBSERVING LAWS THAT AREN'T ENFORCED?
MOST PEOPLE SKIRT THE LAW WHERE THEY CAN.
EVEN A TEN-YEAR MEMBER OF THE UNION, SHOULD HE BECOME PRESIDENT OF THE COMPANY, WOULD AT LEAST CONSIDER OBSTRUCTING IT.
DON'T THINK YOU'RE ANY DIFFERENT.
WHEN YOUR POSITION CHANGES, YOUR PERSPECTIVE ALSO CHANGES.

부진노동상담소
SO...
YOU WANT TO STRENGTHEN YOUR COMPANY'S UNION, IS THAT RIGHT?
YES.
MR. LEE... YOU'RE A MANAGER.
YOUR JOB'S NOT BEING THREATENED, SO WHY ARE YOU DOING THIS?
...
THIS ISN'T SOMETHING THAT CAN BE FIXED SOLELY WITH ONE'S SENSE OF JUSTICE.
YOU SHOULD REALLY REFLECT ON IT BEFORE YOU MAKE A FINAL DECISION.

I'VE THOUGHT ABOUT IT ENOUGH.
IT MAY SEEM LIKE THEY'RE OUT FOR YOUR BLOOD RIGHT NOW, BUT WHAT DO YOU THINK WILL HAPPEN AS THE FIGHT DRAGS ON?
"WHAT A GREAT MAN."
"ALL RIGHT. YOU'VE DONE ENOUGH."
"WE'VE THOUGHT ABOUT IT, AND..."
"...LET'S GIVE YOU A PROMOTION!"
"WE CAN MOVE YOU TO ANOTHER DEPARTMENT, IF YOU'D LIKE!"
"IF IT'S MORE CONVENIENT, WE CAN SET YOU UP AT ANOTHER BRANCH!"
AH... HOW SWEET!

AND IF THEY TAKE YOU OUT OF THE PICTURE, THE WHOLE THING WILL DISSOLVE.
I'M NOT A PERSON WHO CAN STOMACH BRIBES.
I GET IT. SOO-IN LEE IS A GOOD PERSON...
A GREAT PERSON...
YOU'RE ONLY DOING THIS TO AVOID BEING THE BAD GUY.
WHAT WOULD YOU HAVE DONE IF THAT DISMISSAL ORDER HADN'T BEEN GIVEN TO YOU?
YOU'D HAVE JUST PRETENDED NOT TO NOTICE, RIGHT?
AM I WRONG?
YOU CAN'T CLEAN A TOILET WHILE AVOIDING ALL THE SHIT.
FIGHTING REQUIRES MORE THAN JUST YOUR RESOLVE.

I'VE MET A LOT OF PEOPLE LIKE YOU...
...WHO CAN'T STAND GETTING THEIR HANDS DIRTY.
I'M PREPARED TO.
YOU BELIEVE THAT, BUT I DON'T.
YOU HAVE NOTHING TO LOSE IN THIS FIGHT.
THEREFORE, IT'S NOT YOUR FIGHT TO LOSE.
I DON'T INTEND ON RISKING THE LIVELIHOOD OF FOURMIS' EMPLOYEES TO PROTECT YOUR PRIDE...
...SO SAVE YOUR EFFORTS AND WALK AWAY.

HEY, DID I HEAR YOU GOT LAID OFF AGAIN?
THAT COMPANY'S CRAZY.
THEY GOT RID OF US BEFORE EVEN ATTEMPTING TO BARGAIN.
SO HOW'S EVERYBODY FEELING?
IT'S STILL MANAGEABLE, BUT... SOME PEOPLE ARE BLAMING THE UNION FOR THE CUTS...
AND WHAT DO YOU HAVE TO LOSE?

IF THESE PEOPLE LOSE THEIR FIGHT...
...DO YOU HAVE ANYTHING TO LOSE, MR. GU?
...
WHAT MAKES THIS YOUR BATTLE?
WHAT MAKES YOU THINK I CAN'T FIGHT LIKE YOU DO?

IF THIS WAS GOING TO BE YOUR ANSWER, WHY HAND OUT YOUR BUSINESS CARD TO OUR EMPLOYEES? DIDN'T I RECEIVE IT FOR A SITUATION LIKE THIS?
SHOULD I JUST STAND AROUND AND WATCH PEOPLE BEING PUSHED OUT WITHOUT REASON?!
WOULD YOU BE OKAY WITH THAT?!
BECAUSE I'M NOT!
CAN YOU REMEMBER EVERYTHING I SAID TO YOU?
...?

WELL, UH... "I KNOW YOU'RE A GOOD PERSON, BUT--"
THAT'S NO GOOD!
YOU DON'T PAY ATTENTION TO ANYTHING OUTSIDE OF YOURSELF, BUT YOU WANNA ORGANIZE A UNION?!
SOO-IN LEE...
YOU DON'T HAVE A FRIENDLY RELATIONSHIP WITH YOUR EMPLOYEES, DO YOU?
AH, WELL... YEAH, THAT'S A LITTLE UNCOMFORTABLE...
DO YOU EVER EAT MEALS WITH THEM?
WE AREN'T CLOSE ENOUGH TO...
SO START BY SHARING MEALS WITH THEM.
PEOPLE WON'T LISTEN TO YOU JUST BECAUSE YOU'RE RIGHTEOUS. THEY WANT TO LISTEN TO SOMEONE GOOD. ONE OF THEIR OWN.

I'VE REALLY BEEN CRAVING PORK BELLY LATELY.
HEHEHE. YOU ONLY WANT ANIMAL FLESH? NOT A MAN'S?
HA! I DON'T EVEN REMEMBER WHAT THAT TASTES LIKE...
PAY BETTER ATTENTION TO YO HUSBAND!
OH, DO YOU THINK HE'LL PAY ME BACK?
HEHEHEHE.
?
HEH...EH...
SHUFFLE
CLACK
Go-shin Gu
Soo-in Lee. Let's go on a field trip.
VRRR
VRRR

VEST SLOGAN: "STOP DISCRIMINATION AGAINST TEMP WORKERS"

THESE NASTY BITCHES!!
SECURIT
FUCK YOU!! YOU WANNA DIE TODAY?!!

WHAT... WHAT IS THIS?
WELCOME TO THE REAL WORLD!

WHAT DID YOU SAY?
ARE YOU EVEN HUMAN?!
ARGH!

...
...
BACK OFF,
YOU HIRED THUGS!!
...

ALRIGHT!
WE'VE BREACHED! THIS WAY!
YOU IDIOTS! HOLD THE LINE! KEEP 'EM OUT!
경찰
HEY! WHAT ARE YOU DOING?! WHEN THEY PUSHED US, YOU JUST STOOD THERE, BUT YOU'RE SUDDENLY INVOLVED WHEN WE PUSH BACK?
AREN'T YOU PICKING SIDES?!

MOVE! GET OUT OF OUR WAY!
THIS IS A COPY OF THE MINISTRY OF LABOR'S DECISION ON YOUR USE OF DISPATCHED LABOR!
THIS COMPANY IS PRACTICING ILLEGAL TREATMENT OF DISPATCH WORKERS AND THEN TERMINATING THEIR CONTRACTS WHEN THEY JOIN THE UNION!
UNDER CORRECT PROCEEDINGS, THESE PEOPLE SHOULD BE BROUGHT ON AS FULL-TIME EMPLOYEES!
POLICE AND SECURITY MUST WITHDRAW AND ALLOW THE WORKERS HERE TO DISCUSS THIS ISSUE WITH MANAGEMENT!
HEY, MORON. WHY ARE YOU JUST STANDING THERE?
CAN'T WE GET THESE PEOPLE OUT OF HERE?!
UH... YEAH...
찌익
SLICE

OW...
LOOK AT THIS IDIOT. COME ON...
HEY, YOU!!
WITH THE SCAR!!
...?
?
WHO DO YOU THINK YOU ARE...
...GIVING ORDERS TO THE POLICE?!
ARE YOU A POLICE COMMANDER?!
WHAT AUTHORITY DO YOU HAVE?!

ARE YOU OKAY? IT'S NOT DEEP, IS IT?
AH, NO... IT'S FINE.
WHAT ARE YOU DOING?
AREN'T YOU ON DUTY?
HEH. AND YOU, YOU DUMB BASTARD...
WE DON'T KNOW EACH OTHER, SO LET'S WATCH THE TONE, OKAY? PEOPLE ARE GONNA THINK I'M THE ASSHOLE HERE.
HE'S HURT BECAUSE OF YOU GUYS, NOT BECAUSE OF US.

LISTEN... YOU'RE NOW OUTSIDE THE DESIGNATED PROTEST AREA.
YOU'RE TRYING TO TRESPASS ON PRIVATE LAND WITHOUT PERMISSION.
YOU MUST DISPERSE IMMEDIATELY, OR WE'LL ARREST YOU FOR OBSTRUCTION OF BUSINESS OPERATIONS.
WHAT ARE WE INTERFERING WITH?!
HOW DO YOU KNOW WHETHER WE'RE GOING IN THERE TO DISRUPT OR NOT?!
WE'RE JUST TRYING TO GET TO WORK, AND THE POLICE ARE BLOCKING US!!
THE REAL OBSTRUCTION OF BUSINESS HERE IS BEING DONE BY COMPANY SECURITY AND THE POLICE!!

EVEN AFTER YOU'RE FIRED, ACCESS TO UNION ACTIVITIES IS GUARANTEED!
BLOCKING UNION MEMBERS IS INTERFERING WITH THE UNION'S WORK!
FURTHER, TERMINATION OF CONTRACT DUE TO UNION MEMBERSHIP IS UNFAIR DISMISSAL...
...INTENDED TO NEUTRALIZE THE WORKERS' LEGAL RIGHT TO ORGANIZE!!
IF THE POLICE TRULY PROTECT THE RULE OF LAW, THEN THESE SECURITY MEN SHOULD BE ARRESTED IMMEDIATELY!

YES! ARREST THEM!
WHY DIDN'T YOU STOP THEM WHILE THEY PUSHED, INSULTED, AND HARASSED US?!
THE POLICE ARE SIDING WITH THUGS!!
WE'RE NOT TAKING ANY SIDES HERE. WE'RE ONLY PREVENTING A PHYSICAL CLASH BETWEEN THE PARTIES.
JUST... STANDARD PREVENTION...
ISN'T THIS CLASH OCCURRING BECAUSE THESE CRIMINALS AREN'T BEING PUNISHED?!
AREN'T YOU GOING TO DO YOUR JOB?!
IF YOU REFUSE TO ARREST THEM, I'LL HAVE TO CALL THE POLICE!
WE ARE THE POLICE...
ARE YOU CRAZY OR SOMETHING?
NO.
WHO TOLD YOU TO TURN AROUND? LOOK STRAIGHT AHEAD.
WHY WOULD YOU TAKE ORDERS FROM A CIVILIAN?
YOU INTERESTED IN ANYTHING THAT THUG SAYS?
NO, SIR.

HELLO!
IS THIS 112*?
I'M AT THE SAMJIN CORPORATION... YES, THERE...
*HOTLINE FOR THE KOREAN POLICE
THERE'S A BUNCH OF THUGS BLOCKING EMPLOYEES FROM ENTERING THE BUILDING.
YES, YES. PLEASE COME RIGHT AWAY!
WHY COME TO SOMEONE ELSE'S WORKPLACE AND MAKE A FUSS? TROUBLEMAKERS!
HOW COULD WE HAVE FIRED YOU? YOU WERE NEVER OUR EMPLOYEES IN THE FIRST PLACE!
IF YOU WANT TO FORM A UNION OR PROTEST A GRIEVANCE, REMEMBER THAT WE CONTRACTED YOU FROM HUMAN FIRST! GO TO THEM!
HUMAN FIRST? OTHER THAN ONBOARDING THERE AND RECEIVING A TEXT ABOUT MY DISMISSAL FROM SAMJIN, I HAVEN'T BEEN INVOLVED WITH THEM AT ALL!
WHY HOLD THEM RESPONSIBLE FOR **YOUR** PRACTICES?!

YOU'RE THE ONE WHO HIRED US!
HERE'S A PAY STUB!
IT HAS SAMJIN'S NAME ON IT, SO WHY AREN'T WE SAMJIN EMPLOYEES?
YOU'VE ALREADY BEEN JUDGED TO BE GUILTY OF ILLEGAL LABOR PROCUREMENT!! YOU ARE THEIR EMPLOYER!!
YOU MADE THEM WORK LIKE SLAVES, AND THEN YOU FIRED THEM!!
DON'T HIDE BEHIND THE DISPATCH COMPANY!
OF COURSE, WE'LL FOLLOW THE LAW.
WE'LL PAY THE FINE.
HEY! WHERE ARE YOU RUNNING OFF TO?!

EXCUSE ME...
DID SOMEONE
CALL 112?
?

ANYONE?
MISTER...
MISTER!
MISTER FOURMIS!!
OH, UH... YES?
ARE YOU GOOD AT RUNNING?
차별철폐
YE...ES?
TELL ME YOUR 100 METER TIME.
AH, UH... MY BEST TIME'S 12 SECONDS, BUT THAT WAS A WHILE AGO...
WOW! THAT'S PRETTY GOOD, RIGHT?
IF YOU HAVE TIME, COME SUBMIT FOR THE NEXT PROTEST WITH US!

부 우우웅
VROOM
BEEP 빵
빠 앙
BEEEP
IS THAT WHAT'LL HAPPEN IF FOURMIS UNIONIZES?
MAYBE, MAYBE NOT.
WHY? YOU SCARED?
IF YOU'RE SCARED, GO AHEAD AND STOP HERE.
NO...
I THINK I NEED TO TAKE CARE SO THAT IT DOESN'T GET TO THIS POINT.
DO YOU THINK WE DID IT LIKE THIS BECAUSE WE WANTED TO? AS SOON AS THE UNION FORMED, THEY FIRED EVERYONE!
WHAT COULD WE HAVE DONE DIFFERENTLY?!
...
OH-HO, WHAT A NICE ATMOSPHERE WE HAVE IN HERE!

부 진 경찰서
HEY, OFFICER PARK.
IS THEIR RUNNER HERE YET?
HE'S ON THE WAY.
HOW LONG SHOULD WE KEEP DOING THIS?
IF YOU DON'T LIKE IT, DON'T PROTEST.
A FORMER UNION LAWYER'S BECOME THE PRESIDENT NOW, SO WHY KEEP IT UP LIKE YOU DO?

YOU THINK WE DO THIS ALL THE TIME BECAUSE WE'RE SOME KINDA PERVERTS WHO GET PLEASURE FROM IT?
FIRING PEOPLE FOR UNIONIZING WHILE A UNION LAWYER'S PRESIDENT, AS YOU POINTED OUT...
THAT'S THE PERVERSE THING HERE!!
DO YOU KNOW WHAT THE WAGE GAP RATE BETWEEN SMALL AND LARGE COMPANIES IS RIGHT NOW? IT WAS 94.7% IN 1987!
IT WAS 56% IN 2000... BUT *ANYWAY!*
IF YOU HAD TO WORK YOUR ASS OFF TO RECEIVE HALF A NORMAL SALARY, AND THEN THEY FIRED YOU VIA TEXT MESSAGE, ALL "THANK YOU FOR YOUR HARD WORK ^^;;;" WOULD YOU BE FINE LEAVING IT LIKE THAT?
AND THE COPS ARE PART OF THE PROBLEM!! YOU THINK UNIONS ARE THE SAME AS GANGS?
YOU THINK WE'RE A CRIMINAL ENTERPRISE? WHY ARE YOU SO WORRIED ABOUT WHAT WE'RE DOING? IT'S THE COMPANIES YOU SHOULD WATCH!
CHECK WITH THE INFORMATION DIVISION. THAT'S NOT SOMETHING THE CIVIL SERVICE BRANCH DOES...
부다다다다...
VROOM
AH. LOOKS LIKE THEIR RUNNER'S HERE.

ANOTHER DELIVERY GUY. OOF! HE LOOKS LIKE HE COULD BE PRETTY FAST.
EXCUSE ME... WHY AM I HERE?
OH!
YOU'RE RACING THAT GUY.
THE COMPANY ALWAYS PUTS IN FOR EVENT PERMITS FOR THE SAME TIME AND PLACE AS OURS TO PREVENT US FROM GATHERING.
SO, THE COPS MAKE US RACE AND ACCEPT THE WINNER'S APPLICATION.
THE COMPANY ALWAYS SENDS THESE YOUNG, ATHLETIC DELIVERY GUYS. SHAMEFUL.
THEY DON'T EVEN USE THE PERMIT, JUST SNIPE IT FROM US.
SO, IF YOU LOSE, WE WON'T BE ABLE TO HOLD OUR NEXT PROTEST. GET IT?
ALRIGHT! WE'LL GO AT PRECISELY 8 O'CLOCK. SEE THE CONE OVER THERE? FIRST TO TOUCH IT WINS.
WHO'S THE UNION'S RACER?
RIGHT HERE!
UH...

RELAXING MASSAGE...
HEY, KID. HOW MUCH THEY PAYING YOU?
DO YOU GET PAID EVEN IF YOU LOSE? YOU SHOULD. IF YOU DON'T, YOU SHOULD LET ME KNOW.
GULP
OKAY! BOTH RUNNERS, GET READY!
STARTING THE COUNTDOWN!
LET'S GO, MISTER FOURMIS!
5!
4!

3!
2!
1!
GO!

TWEEE EEE!!
FALSE START! GET BACK HERE!
HEY! KYEONG-JANG PARK! WHAT IS THIS, THE OLYMPICS?
WHAT FALSE START?!
IF YOU CAN'T FOLLOW THE RULES, YOU'LL BE DISQUALIFIED.
WE SHOULDN'T HAVE TO QUALIFY IN THE FIRST PLACE! WE HAVE A RIGHT TO ASSEMBLE!
WHY ALLOW THE COMPANY A CHANCE TO TAKE THAT AWAY?
IF YOU WANT A GATHERING PERMIT, RUN THE RACE PROPERLY...
YOU'RE PLAYING FAVORITES HERE!
WHAT, YOU THINK I TOOK A BRIBE OR SOMETHING? YOU THINK I'M BEING BIASED?
MR. GU...
WELL, IF THE SHOE FITS!
HE'S RIGHT. I JUMPED THE GUN.
...

OKAY, LET'S TRY THIS AGAIN.
5, 4...!
3!
2!
1!
GO!

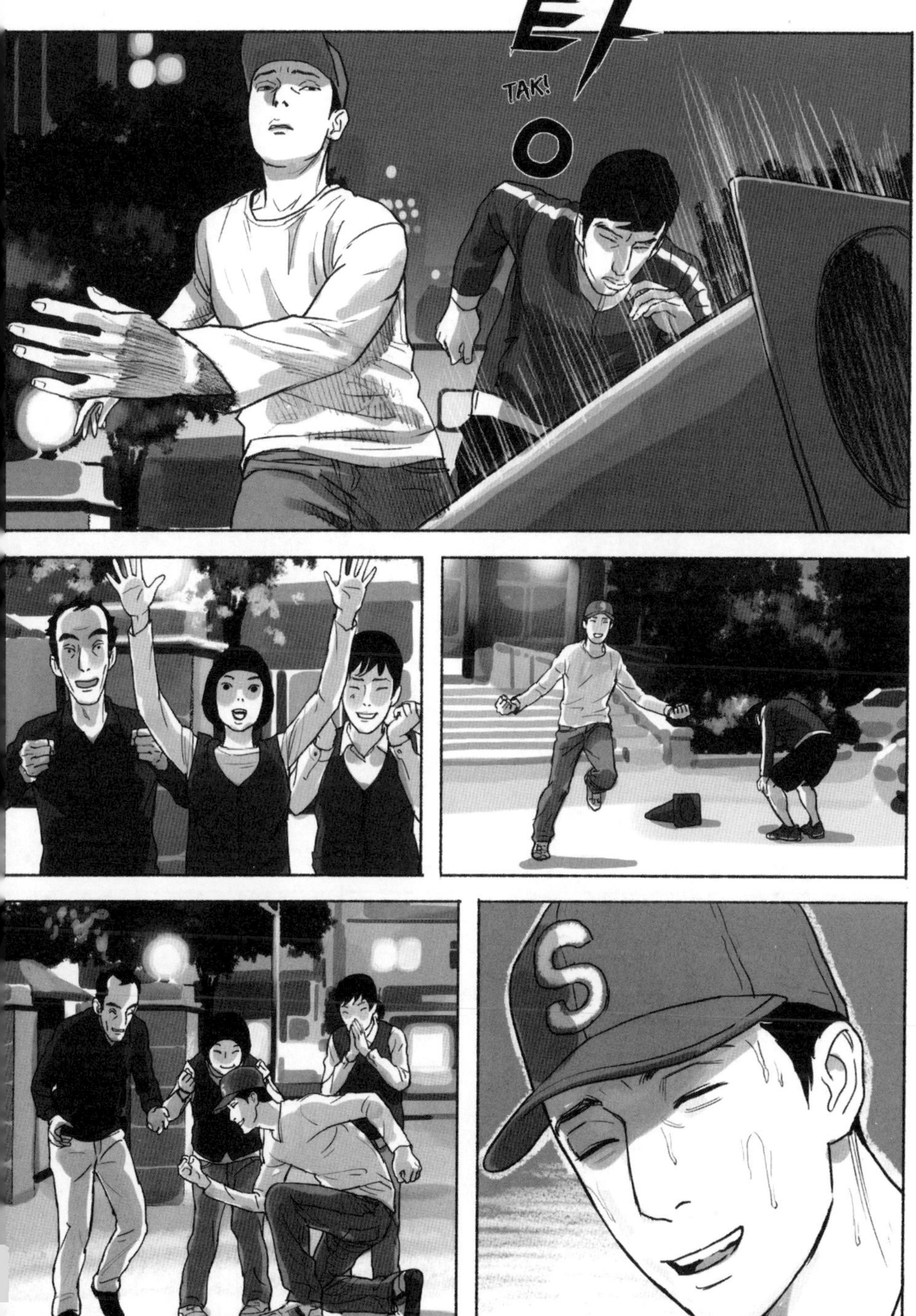
탁
TAK!

SO, WHAT HAPPENED?
OUR APPLICATION'S ACCEPTED THIS TIME, AND THEY'LL ALTERNATE US AND THE COMPANY FROM HERE ON OUT.
WELL, AT LEAST WE DON'T HAVE TO RUN ANYMORE.
SOO-IN, YOU COMING?
WAIT UP, PLEASE. I'LL BE RIGHT BACK.
EXCUSE ME... YOU WERE WORKING AT THE SAMJIN PROTEST EARLIER, RIGHT?
UH, YEAH. THAT'S RIGHT.
THE GUY WHO SLICED HIS HAND OPEN... IS HE OKAY?
...

I DON'T KNOW WHAT YOU'RE TALKING ABOUT.
WHY ARE YOU TRYING TO GET INVOLVED IN POLICE AFFAIRS?
HUH? I JUST WONDERED IF HE'S ALL RIGHT...
I'M WORRIED.
NO ONE WAS INJURED.
YOU'RE GOING TO TELL ME I DIDN'T SEE WHAT I DEFINITELY SAW?
AREN'T YOU HIS COMMANDER? DON'T YOU KNOW WHAT HAPPENED UNDER YOUR WATCH?
HUH...
WHAT DO YOU CARE? ARE YOU A REPORTER OR SOMETHING?
HE'S WITH ME. UNLESS IT'S A BIG, CONFIDENTIAL DEAL, JUST TELL HIM WHETHER THE KID'S ALL RIGHT.

HE WAS AN ARMY CAPTAIN, SO HE'S PROBABLY REMINDED OF HIS OWN SOLDIERS.
YOU WERE A MILITARY OFFICER?
OH. YES.
AFTER EVERYTHING COOLED DOWN, HE WENT TO THE HOSPITAL. HE WASN'T SERIOUSLY INJURED.
AH, THAT'S A RELIEF. THANKS.
WELL, I DIDN'T EXPECT IT, BUT...
...YOU'RE KIND OF A SOFT GUY, HUH?
NEWER RECRUITS VERY OFTEN HAVE TROUBLE SPEAKING UP FOR THEMSELVES, EVEN WHEN THEY'RE HURT...

CONTINUED IN VOLUME 2.

The Awl

The Awl, volume 1
By Choi Gyu-seok
Translation and Lettering: Lynn Eskow

for ablaze

managing editor RICH YOUNG
editor KEVIN KETNER
associate editor AMY JACKSON
designers JULIA STEZOVSKY & RODOLFO MURAGUCHI

This English edition was published by ABLAZE PUBLISHING in 2024 by arrangement with Changbi Publishers, Inc. c/o KCC(Korea Copyright Center Inc.), Seoul and Chiara Tognetti Rights Agency, Milan.

Names: Choi, Gyu-seok, author.
Title: The awl, vol. 1 / Gyu-seok Choi.
Description: Portland, OR: Ablaze, 2023.
Identifiers: ISBN: 978-1-68497-190-9
Subjects: LCSH Executives--Comic books, strips, etc. | Labor unions--Comic books, strips, etc. | Graphic novels. | BISAC COMICS & GRAPHIC NOVELS / Manga / General
Classification: LCC PN6790.K63 .C4613 A95 2023 | DDC 741.5--dc23